ENTER THREE
WITCHES

ENTER THREE WITCHES

Kate Gilmore

Houghton Mifflin Company
Boston 1990

Library of Congress Cataloging-in-Publication Data

Gilmore, Kate.
  Enter three witches / Kate Gilmore.
    p. cm.
  Summary: Bren is fearful of having the girl of his dreams meet his
family of witches, but after a school production of Macbeth which is
attended by his family who cause startling effects, he realizes a
meeting has already taken place.
  ISBN 0–395–50213–6
  [1. Witchcraft–Fiction. 2. New York (N.Y.)–Fiction.]
I. Title.
PZ7.G4374En   1990   89–39560
[Fic]–dc20   CIP
                            AC

Printed in the United States of America

BP 10 9 8 7 6 5 4 3 2 1

For Valerie and Eric

Chapter One

September is a month of mixed emotions — anticipation, hope, and a pang of sorrow for the summer that is suddenly, irrevocably lost. The weather intensifies this sense of a divided heart. One day it's hot enough to swim — but school has just begun. Then a cold rain makes one think of being under the covers with a book. September is sunlight with a little edge, a time when promise and regret mingle, bringing that slight pain in the chest that is almost like fear. And the days run out so fast. To Bren, who would live in Central Park if he had a tent, the shortening afternoons imparted a sensation close to panic.

The small private school on West Eighty-ninth Street ran until four. In many ways Bren liked his shabby, friendly, and often stimulating school. Unfortunately, the last class of the day was economics, and it was held in a room that had a tantalizing view of the street. Through the long windows he could see the light changing on the leafy branches of the plane trees, an agonizing reminder of the passage of time.

1

When the bell finally rang, he dashed for the door, only to stop with a groan as he saw that Eli was going up to Mr. Steiner's desk to ask a question. Eli, his best friend since sandbox days, had funny ideas about how to spend the last hours of a beautiful day.

"Come *on*, Eli," Bren called from the door when the endless question seemed to have been answered. "It's getting dark, you creep."

Eli glanced out at the still glowing afternoon. "So go," he said. "It's not as if I don't know where to find you." But Bren waited, and they walked together toward his house, where they would pick up a Frisbee and a large black dog.

Shadow was a Newfoundland of heroic proportions and a champion Frisbee player, which was fortunate because Eli had a tendency to duck when anything more menacing than a leaf passed through his private air space. Bren knew that Eli would rather be at home, gloating over the microprocessors, converters, and gently humming power supplies that occupied all but a small corner of his bedroom. Instead he went to the park and watched Bren play with his dog.

They reached the place Bren favored for his game. "Why do I do this?" Eli asked, as he tried to find a perch for his bony backside halfway up a small hill, where he hoped the Frisbee would not find him in its murderous horizontal course. "Every day I ask myself the same question, and every day I come up with the same answer: Eli Wilder, you must be crazy."

"It's my magnetic personality," Bren said. "Here you go, Shadow, old boy. First an easy one. Get your reflexes tuned up."

A practiced flick of the wrist, and the Frisbee sailed under the autumn trees, in and out of the golden shafts of light that fell on the worn grass of Central Park. A hundred yards away the great dog crouched, his muscles taut but still, no motion wasted until the last second, when a single economical leap and snap of massive jaws secured the prize.

The game had a theme with only two variations. Sometimes Shadow brought the Frisbee to Bren. Sometimes he pranced away with it, tail wagging, brown eyes shining with mischief.

"Here! Stop, thief! Give me that, you monster," Bren shouted. "Come on, Eli. Don't just sit there. Head him off."

With a sigh, Eli closed his book, dived down the hill, and wrestled Shadow to the ground. "You could train this beast better," he said, as Bren came panting to the fray. "Train him better or find a more athletic friend."

"More athletic than you, or more athletic than Shadow?" Bren asked.

"Than me, you nit. When I think that I could be listening to the Ninth and finishing those circuits."

"Eli," Bren said, crouching with one arm over the dog's dusty shoulders, "Eli, my friend, think. Winter is coming. You can wire circuits till your eyes drop out, but *this* can't last." Bren made an expansive gesture at the autumn glory of the park and fell over in the grass. Eli laughed. Shadow barked and jumped on top of Bren.

Back on his feet, Frisbee in hand, Bren paused and looked with disapproval at the fading light. "You see," he said, "it's almost gone. Every day a few minutes less, and now, oh blast! I think she's calling me."

Eli waited while the familiar look of concentration possessed Bren's face. Shadow, too, appeared to listen to a voice that only they could hear.

After a moment Bren shook his head and gave an exasperated sigh. "Well, that's it for today, I guess. I told her not to call, I'd come when the sun went down, but she can't resist."

"Mothers are like that," Eli said. "I'm just glad mine is limited to the distance she can screech."

"You don't have a clue how lucky you are," Bren said, as they turned toward home. "I'm getting too old for this."

"Maybe you could have a serious talk with her," Eli suggested, not very optimistically. "Ask her to save it for real emergencies or something like that."

"I can try, but it's a bit like reasoning with some force of nature, you know — like maybe a volcano?"

Eli grinned and nodded. He had known Bren and also Bren's mother for a very long time, and he was aware that there was little more to be said on the subject of Miranda West. They walked in companionable silence toward the western edge of the park, where tall apartment towers were silhouetted against a pale sky streaked with apricot.

Chapter Two

Miranda West gazed out the window of her tower room, letting her mind relax from the intense concentration of calling her son. Lights were coming on in the row of brownstones across the street, but half a block away the treetops at the edge of the park were still flooded with late afternoon sunlight. Bren would be on his way now. Miranda hadn't the slightest doubt that she had reached him. This was how it had always been. But he's growing up, she thought, a little uneasily. Will I always be able to call him? Will I want to?

A silvery Siamese cat was watching her from the other side of the window seat, stone still, only the dark tip of its tail twitching, betraying some feline anxiety having to do, perhaps, with dinner. "Come, Luna," Miranda said. "Suppertime for you and then for the hungry horde. So much to do, and here I sit." Suddenly animated, she crossed the room, her long skirt sweeping the intricate figures of the pentagram inlaid in the floor. Behind her the cat, hungry but cautious, circled the magic signs and padded after her down the stairs.

The parlor door was open, and Miranda glanced inside. Her mother's crystal ball glowed softly in its alcove, but the

5

room was empty. "That's good," she said to the cat. "With any sort of luck, she's started dinner."

The kitchen occupied the entire back of the house. Most people in space-hungry New York would have made four rooms of Miranda's kitchen, but the West family loved and needed it just as it was. Huge, dark, inconvenient, it was also welcoming. Copper gleamed on the shadowy walls; rosy fruit and yellow cheese beckoned from the round oak table. In all but the hottest weather a fire burned on the hearth, and often there was something simmering in the kettle that swung on a chain over the flames. There were good smells, too — old-fashioned smells of home-cooked food from the cast-iron range and sometimes just a whiff of something strange floating from the cauldron over the fire.

Miranda's mother, Rose, stood at the stove. She was a plump old lady whose pink cheeks and white hair disguised a snappish temper and a rather dark outlook on life. Many years of professional fortunetelling had not improved her opinion of the human race, and sometimes this view extended to her immediate family.

She glared suspiciously at her daughter's flowing skirts. "Next time it's royalty to dinner you might let me know," she said. "I'll have me hair done up and throw another turnip in the pot."

"Just Bob," Miranda said, leaning over to sniff the curls of steam that rose from the stove. "Mmmm, good, but we'll have to think of something else. Men don't like the soup-and-salad supper. They feel cheated, no matter how full they get. Even Bren, I think, wants something he can get his teeth into."

"Bob, Bob," the old woman muttered. "Let Bob eat quiche.

6

Let Bob stop off for marinated mandarin mushrooms. There's a chicken. Scrawny. You do something with it if you want to."

"Bren needs to see his father," Miranda said, peering into the refrigerator. It was a huge one, set into the wall — the kind that had been an icebox and was now uncertainly supplied with power by an antiquated gas motor.

"Bah! Malarky!" her mother said. "Bren can see his father anytime he wants to. It's you wants to see Bob West, though what you ever saw in that pie-faced yuppie beats me."

"Well, of course I want to see him," Miranda said. She held the chicken up to dubious inspection in the dim light. "The separation wasn't my idea, and I still think I'll get him back, although it's turning out to be harder than I thought it would be. Certainly not if we starve him to death, though. Isn't this an awfully tiny chicken?"

"It'll have to do," Rose said. She snatched the chicken from her daughter and attacked it with a knife. "Maybe when your star roomer, God's gift to the Bulgarian opera, pays her rent, we can have a proper meal."

"Oh, Mama, stop it," Miranda said, laughing. "We're not dependent on poor Madame for our meals. Are we short of money? I'll ask Bob for some more, but don't nag Madame. You know what a hard time she has."

"Let her sell some of the crown jewels we're always hearing about. The ones people kept throwing onto the stage."

"Don't be mean," Miranda said. "Here, let me have the neck for Luna. She's been such a good girl."

They heard the front door slam and a series of thumps, as of things being dropped progressively down the long central hall. "Bren's here," Miranda said. "There, Luna dear. Take it someplace safe."

7

The cat snarled and retreated with its chicken neck under the skirts of the couch, which was one of the kitchen's amenities. She was just in time, for Shadow was, as always, only inches behind Bren.

He seems to bring the park in with him, Miranda thought, smiling at her son. His hair was the color of oak leaves in the fall, and his eyes, above high cheekbones dusted with oak-brown freckles, were gray and green — changeable eyes like an autumn sky.

"Hi, Mom. Hi, Gram. Oh, that smells good. What is it?" Bren leaned over the simmering pot.

"Potato soup," Rose said. "Your father's coming, so I made something special. The strychnine goes in last."

"Dad's coming? Fabulous!" Bren said. "What's the occasion, or is there one?"

"I just thought it would be nice," Miranda said. "You haven't seen him in a while, so I summoned him."

"You *summoned* him?" Bren was incredulous. "You *summoned* Dad?"

"By telephone," Miranda said.

"Whew!" Bren threw himself onto the couch, then hastily pulled up his feet as a furious growling hiss came from beneath. "I don't know why," he went on, "I just don't like the idea that Dad can be summoned. It's out of character."

"It's biologically impossible," Rose said. "When mind calls to mind, there has to be a mind at both ends."

"Mother," Miranda said, drawing herself up to her considerable height and glaring down at the old woman, "I am really tired of this. Bren loves his father, and I am still fond of him. You might also remember who supports this menagerie. Not the mad diva in the attic, as you have pointed out,

8

but not you and your tea leaves either. Not by a long shot. So just remember which side your bread is buttered on, or I'll curdle your soup."

Bren viewed this scene with admiration. His mother's beauty was enhanced by rage, a fact of which she was happily unaware. Her mane of fair hair seemed to crackle with malevolent energy, and her blue eyes burned in the pale perfection of her face. Shadow left his bowl of dog food and came to lay his head on Bren's knee. "It's all right, old boy," Bren said, stroking the sleek, black head. "She won't look at us like that. Not so long as we're good, so try to be a model dog. Don't leave your toys on the stairs, don't spill your water, don't . . ."

"Oh, Bren," Miranda said, laughing. "It's not that bad. I'm not even that mad at my dear old mum, and if I spoiled her soup, what would we do for dinner? I could hardly ask her to make another."

"Irish," Rose muttered. "Kill you one minute, kiss you all to pieces the next."

"You should talk," Miranda said.

The doorbell rang. Bren and Shadow tore out of the kitchen and down the hall to admit Bob West to his former home.

"Hey, Dad. This is *all right*," Bren said. "Down, Shadow, you brute. He's glad to see you too."

"Hey, Bren. What's new besides the fact that this dog needs to go to school?" Bren's father shoved the Newfoundland adroitly in the chest with a well-tailored knee and thumped his son on the back.

"I'll take him soon," Bren promised. "This winter for sure. Those classes are held indoors, Dad."

Bob laughed and started down the hall. "So how's life in the zoo?" he asked.

"Terrific," Bren said. "If we had a man around the house, it would be perfect."

Bob pulled up short by the kitchen door. "You know where to find me," he said.

Bren looked uncomfortable and bent a little away from his father to scratch Shadow's ears. "Yeah, I know, but I'm sorry, Dad. I really like it here, strange as that may seem."

"So okay. Back to square one, as usual," Bob said. "Let's go see what the ladies have brewed for supper. I'm sure that's the right word."

Miranda stood by the oak table, where the Tiffany lamp cast its fragmented rainbow onto her white silk shirt. She was holding a bottle of distinguished Scotch. "Well, I didn't brew this, at least," she said.

"Extravagant woman. Now I know where all the money goes." Bob poured himself a sizable drink and waved the bottle at the rest of them. "Anybody else? It's the real thing." They shook their heads. "Maybe this explains our incompatibility," he went on after a long, appreciative swallow. "Failure to enjoy good booze is a serious flaw in a woman's character."

"It interferes," Miranda murmured. "One needs such a clear head in my line of work."

"How could I forget?" Bob asked, and headed for the couch.

"Watch your ankles," Bren cried. "Luna's got her dinner under there."

His father deposited his drink on the table and lifted one end of the couch to disclose a furious Siamese. "Come out of there, hellcat," he said. "I'm damned if I'll stand all night for disgusting Luna. Out! I said." The cat seized its chicken neck and fled under the stove.

"You be careful, stupid white man," said a voice from the doorway. "Don't you mess with Luna. She got the power too, and don't you forget it." A formidable black woman stood just inside the kitchen door and glared at Bob West, who let the couch down with a thump.

"Aha!" he cried. "Louise LaReine. Queen Lou. Another unforgettable character from my former life. How you doin', sweetheart? I didn't know you were still gracing this mansion with your irresistible charms."

The woman pointed dramatically at the shining tile floor. "Who you think scrub these tile?" she demanded. "Who scrape the crud off that stove? Not her ladyship, I promise you." She cast a glance, in which malevolence and affection were curiously mixed, at Miranda, who was looking amused.

"Stow it, Louise," Bob said. "Miranda could rent that hole of yours for eight hundred bucks — black feathers, cock's blood, and all. A thousand, if she cleaned it up. That's what's called a garden apartment these days, and you can get a lot of expert maid service for that kind of dough."

"She better not try," Louise said. "She try that kind of crap on me, and we just see which be stronger — white witchery or good old black obeah."

"Louise, dear, be calm," Miranda said. "He's only teasing. I haven't the least interest in a trial of strength or in losing your invaluable services. Don't pay him any mind."

Possibly mollified, the black woman snorted and left as suddenly as she had come.

"You insulted her," Miranda said.

11

"I meant to," Bob answered. "I insulted her regularly when I lived here, and I see no reason to be more civil now that I don't. The woman is loathsome. How you can even think about what she does with those black chickens she keeps in the garden, much less listen to their strangled cries, is more than I can imagine."

"I don't hear any strangled cries," Miranda said, "and I have always believed in professional tolerance. Let's talk about something more agreeable. Mama, how's the soup?"

"Somebody had better set the table," Rose said, "or there won't be any place to put the soup."

"Bren," said his father, "you have been elected by popular acclaim."

"Why me?" Bren grumbled. "I can't tell right from left. The minute I look at silverware and napkins, my mind goes blank."

"You get the stuff. I'll straighten it out," Bob said.

Miranda watched fondly as they set the table. They look so alike, she thought, the boy a more refined version of the man, both tall and brown-haired with regular, suntanned features. Even their eyes were the same color, yet that was where the difference lay. Bob's were the eyes of a good-looking, confident, self-satisfied man; nothing more. In Bren's there was another quality, an animal awareness and a disturbing depth. He's *mine*, she said to herself, and went to serve the soup.

Dinner was fairly amicable. "This is good, Rose," Bob said after a reflective sip. "You always had a hand with soup."

"Comes of having to make do," the grandmother said.

"People who always have meat on the table forget how to make a good soup."

"Peasant virtue?" he said. "How long has it been since you had to go without meat?"

"Wait till you see the chicken she expects me to divide into four."

"Just so it didn't come from the back yard," Bob said.

"I would never take one of Louise's chickens," Miranda said. "They don't look very sanitary, for one thing, and there would be repercussions of a most unpleasant kind."

"Not to change the subject," Bren said, and then stopped. He had wanted to avoid another round in the ongoing argument about Louise LaReine and her curious practices, but hadn't yet thought of a new topic. Everyone looked at him expectantly. "Eli wants me to help him light a play this fall," he said at random. "I thought it might be fun. We've got such a neat theater."

"No gym, no sports facilities of any kind, but a neat theater," Bob complained. "That's a New York school for you."

"Well, Dad, if a monstrously rich athlete had graduated from Perkins instead of a monstrously rich actor, we would probably have a gym and no theater," Bren said. "It was just a matter of chance."

"What play?" Miranda asked.

Bren hesitated. "*Macbeth*," he said finally.

"Oh, Lord, not old bubble, bubble, toil and trouble," Rose said. "What a bore. They'll get it all wrong."

"Maybe I can be a consultant," Miranda suggested.

This struck Bren as a truly horrible idea. "There's a lot

more to *Macbeth* than witches," he said. "In fact, I think the witches are sort of minor."

"There, you see? What did I tell you?" Rose said. "Minor indeed."

"Gramma, I haven't even read the play yet," Bren protested. "It's just an impression I have — that the witches are more or less local color. What do you think, Dad?"

"Sorry, old boy. I had that stuff in school, but it all went in one ear and out the other."

"The witches," Miranda explained, "appear briefly, but they are hugely important. They not only foretell the events of the play, they actually make things happen because the characters believe their prophecies and act accordingly. Besides, Shakespeare was full of wonderful witch lore and witch language."

"And it all takes place on a blasted heath," Rose said. "Twisted trees, drifting mists. What more could one ask? But, as I said, they'll probably muck it up."

"It sounds like fun to light," Bren said. "Not that I know much about lighting, but Eli does. He's a wizard with anything electrical."

"*Is* he?" Miranda asked.

"Not the way you mean," Bren said.

They were now well into the chicken, which had been stewed in tiny pieces with many vegetables to stretch it. It was delicious, and Bren had a warm feeling in his stomach that came even more from the apparent truce between his parents. He continued to hope that his father would abandon his bleak and expensive apartment on the other side of the park and come back to the house on West Eighty-fourth Street. Bob and Miranda were in the uncomfortable position

14

of people who love each other but can't stand to live together. Only the mysterious power of sexual attraction, assisted in this case by a touch of the supernatural, could explain how they had ever made it through as many years of marriage as they had.

Shortly after dinner, however, Bob rose to go, pecking his estranged wife on the cheek and giving Bren another manly punch on the arm. "Call me this weekend, and maybe we can kick a ball around in the park — you and me and the IBM," he said. Bren looked puzzled. "The immense black monster," Bob explained and left, laughing.

Rose looked at the clock. "Put the dishes in the sink," she said. "Maybe if we grovel, Louise will do them tomorrow. I've got a client."

"At this unholy hour?" Miranda asked.

"Exactly at this unholy hour. This woman is so superstitious she'd come on the stroke of midnight, if I gave her a chance. Happily, she pays extremely well." The old woman took up a Spanish shawl and wrapped herself in its gaudy folds.

"Spirits or futures?" Miranda inquired languidly as she started to pick up the dishes.

"One never knows," Rose said. "It depends on what the stars have told her to do on the day in question."

"Don't laugh at the stars, Mother."

"Laugh? I don't laugh at anything, but this woman is a fool. There's the bell."

Rose stamped away to the front door, and Bren helped his mother clear the table. "I wouldn't want her to tell my fortune," he remarked. "I'm sure it would be full of scorpions and ugly girls and death by water and all that terrific stuff."

"Your grandmother is one hundred percent honest," Miranda said. "If she sees scorpions and ugly girls, scorpions and ugly girls is what you'll get." She filled a kettle and put it on the stove so that she and Bren could have tea by the fire as they sometimes did when they were alone.

Bren turned out all the lights except the Tiffany lamp, which shed its multicolored glow on the shadowy walls. "Just the same, I'm not going to ask," he said.

Miranda poured tea, and they pulled their chairs closer to the fire. "Fortunately, you don't have to, as you perfectly well know," she said. "Mother and I did a complete job on you when you were born — horoscope, crystal, auguries, even your tiny palm — and everything was absolutely rosy. You're fortune's child, all right, but you still have to make something of yourself."

Bren had heard this before, or most of it. "Auguries?" he asked. "What kind of auguries? This is a new one to me."

Miranda looked faintly guilty. "Well, we didn't want to leave any stone unturned," she said.

"You mean like sheep's entrails?" Bren asked, wrinkling his nose. "That kind of thing?"

"We subcontracted that part to Louise," Miranda admitted.

"Boy, I'll bet Dad was just crazy about that."

"He didn't know," Miranda said.

For a time they were silent, the firelight playing on their contented faces.

Finally Bren said, "Listen, Mom, I don't want you to take this the wrong way. I would always want you to call me if there were any kind of emergency, but do you think you could let up on these routine, come-home-to-dinner calls? I guess I like to think I can look at a clock or notice that it's getting dark and just come like anyone else — maybe even forget sometimes or decide I'll stay a little longer. You know?"

Miranda studied him for a moment. Then she said, "When I call, you feel really *compelled*? As if you're not free to choose?" Bren nodded, and she frowned. "That's funny. That's not the way it's meant to be, or is it? I honestly don't know."

"Of course, that's the way it's meant to be," Bren said, a little impatiently. "It's the power thing."

"I guess so," Miranda said. "There ought to be two kinds of calling, then. I'll work on that."

"You work on it, if you want to," Bren said, "but just let me decide for myself that it's time to come home. Do you mind a lot?"

"No. I don't think so," his mother said reluctantly. She stretched one long, white hand out toward her son. An intricate gold ring with a dark stone winked in the firelight before she thought better of it and withdrew the gesture. "I suppose I'm testing you," she said in a burst of honesty. "It makes me feel good to know I can still do it."

"You'll always be able to call me," Bren said. "I'm sure of it."

"Do you mind?" she asked.

"What if I do?" Bren said. "Is there some sort of remedy for having a witch for a mother? I'm sorry. That sounds worse than I meant."

"Maybe you should go live with your father after all," Miranda snapped. "Get away from all this evil influence."

"Oh, stop it," Bren said. "You know I don't want to live in that little brick box when I've got all this, and besides, I'm sure your powers stretch quite a lot farther than the east side of the park. What would be the point?"

"Go and find out," Miranda said furiously. "I won't call you. I promise."

"Mom!" Bren shouted, jumping to his feet. "I don't *want* to go, okay? I *like* it here. I love you and Gram and our horrible tenants and even Luna when she's not biting me. So cut it out."

"I'm sorry, Bren," Miranda murmured. "I'm being a controlling mother. Let's start over. How's your tea? I could warm it up."

Bren sat down with an exasperated sigh. "My tea is fine, Mom. And don't worry about being controlling. I'm sure you can help it even less than most mothers."

"You're so understanding for your age, Bren."

"Sure. Thanks," Bren said. He put his feet up on the hearth and sipped his tea. Over the crackling of the fire came a weird, chromatic keening that seemed to originate in the chimney.

"She really shouldn't practice this late," Miranda said. "The neighbors will complain."

"We can probably hear her better than anybody else," Bren said. "Lucky us. Is she really under the delusion that somebody might pay her to sing?"

"She just does what's important to her, like all the rest of us," Miranda said, "and then, of course, there's the added fact that she really is quite mad, poor thing."

"Bonkers," Bren said. "She told me the other day that Caruso was her singing coach."

"But Bren, that's quite possible, given her age."

"He's coaching her *now*, Mom," Bren explained.

18

"Oh, that is a bit wide of the mark."

"You could say so."

They had returned to their usual state of somnolent comfort, but now the front door slammed, and Rose's quick step was heard in the hall. Bren got up and stretched. "Bedtime," he said, and gave his mother a light tap on the head. "Ta, Mum. Thanks ever so for the char. Come, Shadow."

"If you're going to go on sleeping with that dog, we'll have to get you a bigger bed," Miranda said.

"I'm practicing for sleeping with a woman," Bren said from the door. "A short, fat woman who snores. Night, Gram." He passed his grandmother and headed for the stairs to his room.

Chapter Three

During the night the wind changed, carrying the golden weather out to sea, bringing a sky that looked more like November. Bren gazed with disapproval at the clouds brooding over the dark faces of the brownstones across the street. During breakfast rain started to hiss down the chimney. Bren grumbled so much about the weather that Miranda offered to change it for him. Bren said he thought efforts as drastic as that should be saved for more important occasions. It was, after all, a school day. Let her save her strength for the weekend.

By the time school was over, things had gone from bad to worse, and Eli suggested that they should go down to the theater and monkey with the lights. They got the key from Mr. Behrens, swearing many oaths of responsibility so he would leave and let them have the place to themselves.

Edward Behrens wanted to go home, where he would put his feet up, play some progressive jazz, and study *Macbeth*. He was a new teacher of physics and chemistry — and astronomy, when he could squeeze it in. He also coached the drama club in what was laughingly called his spare time. For all of this he was paid extremely poorly, but he had a lot of fun. He was young, heavily bearded, and very large. The students, inevitably, called him Edward Bear.

"I let a girl go down already," Mr. Behrens said. "The new dancer who's so smart, what's her name? Erika. Said she wanted to try out some steps, so I let her go on the grounds that anyone who could do physics *and* dance couldn't be all bad."

"That's fine," Eli said. "I like having someone on the stage. I'll turn her purple, pink, and pistachio."

"Enjoy," Mr. Behrens said, and ducked out into the rain.

Eli led Bren down into the double basement, which had been widened and deepened under the two old West Side houses that comprised the Perkins School. Here a grateful alumnus, who had learned to act among the pushed-back tables of the school cafeteria, had spent a great deal of money and created a little gem of a theater. In the balcony was a booth with a small but wonderfully sophisticated lighting switchboard, the object of Eli's deepest love and, until now, a complete mystery to Bren. Eli turned on a shaded lamp and ran an experienced eye over the array of dials and switches. "Nothing on but work lights now," he remarked, and Bren nodded sagely. Neither of them bothered to glance out the long window that ran across the front of the booth, giving a view of the stage where a slim girl in a leotard was dancing in the cold, gray light. "That's this switch here," Eli said, flipping it off. A banshee howl of rage came from the dark stage. "Oh, sorry, lady," Eli muttered. "Let's see. We'll give her something special from the last show. If no-

21

body screwed around with the program over the summer." He consulted a long cue sheet from last spring's production of *The Tempest*.

"You'd better hurry," Bren suggested, as a stream of unladylike language rose from the stage.

Eli punched a few buttons and began to turn a dial. The abusive comments stopped, and Bren looked out over the rows of seats to the bare platform, where a magic transformation was taking place. Softly from the wings came a mist of midnight blue, and then a ghostly pale green touched a fragment of scenery upstage. The girl was a black silhouette, arrested against the growing backdrop of light. Now a white beam began to shine from somewhere above their heads. She stepped into it, and her short, wild hair flamed in the sudden illumination. Eli's fingers played again over the controls, and gradually the lighting grew less harsh. Pinks and light ambers filled in the shadows where the girl had begun once more to dance.

"So, okay, now this is lesson one," Eli began. "The changes for that scene were programmed into the board so that when the cue came up, all I had to do was . . . Hey, Bren. You want to learn how to do this stuff or you want to stare at that skinny girl the rest of the afternoon?"

"I want," Bren said slowly, "to watch that skinny girl for the rest of my life. I'll learn about lighting some other time. Just keep her lit, my dear friend Eli. Just keep her lit."

Eli shook his head and continued to play with his switchboard, doing things that were alternately wonderful and grotesque to the dancing girl, and Bren gazed on. She was not really skinny, he thought. She was small and lithe, some would have said "boyish," but this was not a word that occurred to him. It was hard to tell under the changing lights exactly what color her hair was, but now Bren remembered it. The school was small, and few had failed to note Erika's hair, which was a rather improbable shade of red — more pink than red, perhaps. She wore black jeans, white shirts, and a motorcycle jacket. Not crazy enough to be punk, but with a touch of that. She was definitely a girl with her own style and a defiant way of carrying it off. In black tights and leotard she was, to Bren, wrenchingly beautiful.

Eli was leaning around him to see the cue sheet. "Hey, Bren," he said. "You want to stare, go stare someplace else. This place is too small for useless baggage. Go play a scene with Juliet down there. Yeah, that's an idea: I'll light you both." Eli chortled, and Bren looked horrified. "You mean like go up on the stage and talk to her?"

"Something stupid like that I had in mind," Eli said, "but do what you want so long as you don't do it in here."

To go and sit in the empty theater, an audience of one, seemed even more difficult than a confrontation with the girl on the stage. Bren compromised by going down to the front of the house and looking up at her.

Erika stopped dancing. "Hi, down there," she said. "Who are you? I can't see a thing with these lights in my eyes."

"Bren West," Bren said.

"Are you responsible for all those neat effects?"

"No, that was Eli. He's still at it," Bren added, as Erika changed from a golden girl to a purple one.

"I see what you mean," she said. "Come on up here and share the spotlight with me, as the saying goes." Erika gave a low laugh — more of a gurgle than a laugh, an enchanting sound.

23

Bren scrambled up onto the stage, and Eli, who was obviously anticipating the moves in this improvised drama, skewered them both with white spotlights.

"Don't mind him," Bren said, turning to glare at the light booth.

"No, I love it," Erika said. "Don't you? I mean you can't imagine how performers feel about lights. I guess that's obvious, but really, lights can be absolute magic. Who's lighting *Macbeth*, do you know?"

Bren found that his interest in stage lighting had suddenly revived. "Eli and I," he said. "Why? Are you in it?"

"First witch!" she said proudly.

"That's terrible," Bren said. "I mean, a witch — you don't look like a witch. Not like that kind of witch."

"What kind of witch do I look like?" Erika wanted to know.

"Forget it," Bren said. "You don't look like any kind of witch."

"Do I look like Lady Macbeth?"

"I don't know what Lady Macbeth should look like."

"Stately and menacing," said Erika, stretching herself up to her full five feet and pulling a long face.

"Well, but a witch . . ." Bren said helplessly.

"Bren, the witches are fabulous. Eli, some witch lights, please!" Erika shouted, and Bren jumped. Her normal speaking voice was low, with an intriguing trace of huskiness. Her shout was something else again.

"Give me a minute on that," came Eli's faint voice from the booth.

"He's using cues from *The Tempest*," Bren said, squandering in one sentence his entire knowledge of stage lighting. "There ought to be something good in that."

24

Erika made a horrible face and dropped to all fours. "Caliban lights," she said, bounding over to Bren and gazing up at him with what was suddenly the look of an ugly but appealing monster. "Caliban lights would be just fine." The stage darkened again, and out of the wings came shafts of icy green and blue. Erika ran her hands through her hair, which had turned pitch black, changing it into a spiky bush. There were great black shadows on her white face, and her body was all angles, emaciated but somehow strangely attractive. She began a slow, perversely fascinating dance.

"Fair is foul and foul is fair. Hover through the fog and filthy air," chanted Erika as she circled an imaginary cauldron.

Bren watched with a mixture of consternation and delight. Witches, he thought. It had to be witches, didn't it? And even the immense distance that separated the ladies of his household from Shakespeare's savage grotesques did not seem great enough. Apart from this, he was happy. A whole new world was opening before his eyes as he gazed at the dancing girl. He would learn stage lighting and take a major part in the production of *Macbeth*. If Erika enjoyed playing a witch, he would make her a weirdly beautiful one. After rehearsals he would walk her home and they would stop off in one of the West Side's innumerable little cafés.

Suddenly Bren had an inspiration — one so full of terror and promise, it made the hair rise on the back of his neck. In three days there would be one final event in the summer's long cultural spree at the Delacorte Theater in Central Park. A dance recital.

But I hardly know her, he thought, as Erika performed one last contortion and came to stand, radiant and breathless, before him. Eli, out of some unaccustomed kindness, or by accident, changed the lighting to a flattering, late afternoon glow.

"Well, at least you can sort of see what I mean," she said. "And the witch scenes will be a real challenge. I can't wait."

"We'll do something amazing with the lights," Bren promised. He hoped that Eli would still have him, and even more that Eli would not decide to come down from the light booth to discuss the show. In this his luck held, but Erika seemed about to escape.

"Great," she said. "I'll expect it. Some special effects, too — smoke, lightning. I've got to dash. 'Bye for now."

I can ask her in physics tomorrow, Bren thought. And worry about it all night? No thanks. "Hey, Erika!" he called to her retreating back. "Are you going to the dance thing in the park Saturday night?"

She whirled. "No! What dance thing? I didn't hear there was one. Is it any good?"

"The best," Bren said recklessly; he knew next to nothing about dance.

"Then let's go," Erika said. "What a neat idea," and she was gone into the dark wings of the theater.

Bren stared with bulging eyes at the place where she had been. Was it as easy as that? Surely not, but still, it seemed to be. A shared interest (he would have to read everything he could find about dance in the next few days), a convenient event, and presto chango, there you were dating the girl of your dreams. It was like magic, and he had done it himself. Now for Eli. He was going to have to be spectacularly nice to Eli, who would have a heavy teaching job ahead of him.

"Eli," he cried, arriving breathless in the light booth, "I've changed my mind again. Please don't say anything smart; just teach me everything you know about lighting as fast as possible. I want to run the board for *Macbeth*."

Eli grinned. "So now he wants to run the whole show. All of a sudden Mister Big Shot. Don't worry, there's plenty you can do. About the performance, we'll see how many plugs you've rewired. I might let you run a change or two."

"I knew you would," Bren said. "Now show me about these plugs."

"With pleasure," Eli said, and handed him a screwdriver.

Chapter Four

Erika sprinted through the rain. She had pulled a short black skirt and an oversized white turtleneck on over her leotard. Shiny black boots and a red umbrella completed her costume for the rainy afternoon. As she ducked and skipped, her umbrella swerved overhead; once, when she raised it high to get out of someone's way, it struck the branch of a tree and deluged her with raindrops. She laughed and skidded to a stop at Broadway, which was crowded and gleaming under the street lamps, already lit in the early dusk.

Erika's apartment building, the Apthorp, was built in a square with a garden in the middle and tall, wrought iron gates on Broadway and on West End Avenue. The doorman stood under the arch and waved to Erika as she galloped past. He was pleased to see her look so happy. Doormen know everything, and this one disapproved of Erika's father, who left her largely alone in the big apartment overlooking the Hudson River.

She, however, was delighted to be by herself. Once inside the apartment, she shed boots and umbrella on the floor, put an old Stones record on the phonograph, turned the volume up full, and gave herself over to a state of unaccustomed joy.

Rose trudged through the rain with a shopping basket on her arm. The dampness made her bones ache, made her think of dreary things like age and decay and the steady passage of time. She, too, had an umbrella, which she held firmly jammed down over her head. From its shelter she peered gloomily at a glistening display of fruits and vegetables. She reached out and pinched a peach. "Lady, no touch!" cried the Korean grocer, who was watching the fruit.

"I'll touch if I like, and I'll pinch you too, if you don't get some ripe fruit," Rose said.

The Korean made a hasty sign with his hand, a sign that in his country was believed to avert the evil eye.

Shaking her head, Rose turned the corner. There were plenty of these stores to choose from — all beautiful, all useless. "Plastic," she muttered. "Plastic fruit, plastic vegetables." They should sell that monster of a house and go live in the country, where, Rose thought, the food would be scruffy but real. She sighed. Miranda would never move. She was as happy as a flower drifting around the big rooms, dreaming and concocting spells in her lofty studio. And Bren had another year of school. Make the best of it, she thought, and stopped in front of another Korean greengrocer.

Miranda, however, was not particularly happy. She wandered about her room in the twilight and gazed out discontentedly at the rain. Her studio was in the tower which bulged from one corner of the stone mansion. When she and Bob had first moved in, she had chosen this third-floor tower room. It had seemed a snug and, important for a witch, a very private space. Gradually, however, she had come to feel that something was missing — a sense of mystery, a touch of grandeur. It had then occurred to her that perhaps a twelve-foot ceiling was not enough. Finally a pair of baffled workmen had been hired to cut through to the floor above, and now the studio rose twenty feet to the very top of the house. Since the fourth-floor room had been provided with stained glass windows, this renovation produced a curious and gratifying effect. On sunny days the high spaces were washed with multicolored light, but on a dismal evening such as this, they were filled with purple shadows. One could imagine bats and other, less material things.

On an impulse, Miranda went to a cupboard and selected a handful of greenish incense pellets from a tall glass jar. These she placed in the brass thurible that stood on a black table in the center of the room. Then she looked at it long and hard. A thin column of smoke began to rise straight up, then to waver and curl among the shadows above her head. There was a faint, woodland smell of wild strawberries, perhaps, and of something not quite so nice, like toadstools or the undersides of rotting logs.

Returning to the cupboard, Miranda took out a long, thin object wrapped in silk. Carefully she withdrew a black-handled knife inlaid with runes, her athamé or witch's knife. She sprinkled it with salt water from the chalice that stood beside the thurible and then passed it through the low flame. Now with the purified athamé she traced a triangle around the table and made the sign of the cross three times in the air. After lighting two more candles with a match, she sat down with her back to the window and stared into the gilt mirror that stood behind the thurible. She saw her pale face and halo of fair hair reflected against the streaming window glass, and beyond, the vague forms of wind-tossed branches. The candles flickered, and the vision swam in the growing veil of smoke.

"Better," Miranda murmured. "O spirits of the air, I grow bored; I grow stale. Show me there's more to life than dull housewifery!" She closed her eyes for a moment, then opened them again to stare into the mirror. A faint line of blue fire began to play around its frame, and the surface clouded over. Miranda felt her head throb. Then suddenly the mirror grew clear again. As she stared, she lost all awareness of the surrounding room. Slowly, through smoke and wavering flame, through water and leafy branches, a towering figure formed and hovered over the brownstones of West Eighty-fourth Street. Menacing, beautiful — as real as fear, as insubstantial as a dream — it loomed outside Miranda's window, an answer to her longings and also a very considerable fright.

But she would never know what the spirit she had summoned might portend; the spell was broken by the arrival of her only son — the banging door, the joyful barking of the dog. Suddenly she was only a rather beautiful woman gazing into a mirror in an absurdly smoke-filled room on a rainy afternoon.

"O great and holy spirit, I license thee to depart into thy proper place, and be there peace between us evermore by Satandar and Asentacer. So mote it be!" Miranda muttered all in one breath, for she knew the risk of failing to give a spirit permission to leave, even when it might seem to have already done so. She turned and stared out the window at gray rain clouds now darkening ominously into night. Ominous they might be, she thought, but still just clouds. "I'll try that one again," she said, as Bren knocked and entered without waiting for a reply. Shadow was at his heels, bouncing and nudging with his shaggy head.

"Hi, Mom. What will you try again?" Bren said. "Ugh, what a smell. Sit, Shadow. You have to be good in here."

"Hi, sweet," Miranda said, blowing him a kiss. "You're right, it's a horrid smell. I won't use that one again." She opened the window a few inches, and the heavy, green smoke began to creep out into the rainy dusk.

"So what were you up to?" Bren asked. He was wandering around the room, picking things up and putting them down, peering idly at the symbols and calculations on his mother's desk.

"Oh, just a little conjuring and summoning," Miranda said. "I was so bored with those spells for Mrs. Goodrich, and besides, I need a frog."

"All out of frogs?" Bren asked. He looked into the terrarium next to the desk and saw that although there were a number of hopping and crawling things, it was innocent of frogs. "You'll have to think of a substitute."

"You know I can't do that," Miranda said. "It's not like using honey instead of sugar. Frogs are basic, even if they're not so popular as they used to be. Unfortunately, though, Mr. Chu has run out, and I don't want to go to another dealer. What do you think?"

"What do I think? You're asking *me* where to find frogs?" Bren gave the astrolabe a push and watched it rotate slowly on its long chain in the center of the room. "There might be some in Central Park," he said, "but you'd never catch them, and the rangers wouldn't approve. The only other place I can think of is . . . Oh, no. I must be crazy. What a dumb idea."

"The biology lab!" Miranda cried.

"Stop that!" Bren said. "What are you doing, reading my mind?"

"Not at all. It's perfectly logical."

"It's perfectly insane. Put it right out of your mind," Bren said, with the doomed feeling he had whenever he saw that his mother had made up her mind to something he didn't want to do. "I don't take biology this year. The biology teacher's new and I've heard *very* strict about her supplies, pathologically fussy, in fact."

"I hear you, Bren," Miranda said. "I'm not feeble-minded. You just don't want to snitch even one little frog — one little frog that wouldn't be missed. You want me to go all the way downtown and spend a ghastly day trying to get another suspicious Chinese to trust me enough to take my money."

"I'll get the name of the biology supply place," Bren said. "I'll even write the letter."

"That shouldn't take more than a month," Miranda said. "Meanwhile Mrs. Goodrich will certainly find another witch."

Bren laughed and clutched at his head. "You're impossible," he cried. "All right, I'll look. Okay? Just look in the bio lab. No promises, understand?"

"Of course," his mother said. "I wouldn't want you to promise and then do something that might get you in trouble. Just scout around. 'Case the joint,' I think is the phrase."

"That's the phrase," Bren said. "Burglars use it."

"Well, it's not like it's anything valuable. Stop wandering

33

around. Come sit by the window and tell me about your day. You're late. Did you do something after school?" Miranda tucked her feet up on the window seat and beckoned to her son.

"Eli took me to look at the switchboard," Bren explained. "I'm going to help him light *Macbeth*, which will be really cool; but the price I have to pay is doing a lot of electrical work — putting plugs on cables, stripping wires, that sort of thing. I suppose it will come in handy someday."

"Almost certainly," Miranda said. "And then?"

"What do you mean, 'and then?' That's how I spent the time after school. Oh, all right. There was an interesting girl there. She was dancing, and we fooled around, turning her all different colors. She liked that. She's going to play the first witch, and I'm going to take her to the dance program at the Delacorte on Saturday. There. Now you know it all."

Miranda smiled happily. "Well, it's a start," she said. "What kind of dance does she do?"

"Some sort of ballet, I suppose," Bren said. "Everything I know about dancing I learned at parties, and that's not much."

"You'd better go to the library and read up on it."

"Would that help?" he asked. "I doubt it, and when do I have time to go to the library?"

"Books are better than nothing," Miranda said. "Why don't you ask Madame Lavatky? She has tons of books on the performing arts — mostly opera, I suppose, but surely ballet too. She'd be thrilled to lend you one."

Bren groaned. "She's always thrilled to see me, but the feeling is not mutual. Still, it's worth a try. Come, Shadow. Come and defend me for just a minute, and then I'll take you out. Please do something about supper, Mom. I could eat a horse. Or maybe a fat Siamese cat," he added, as Luna slid from under Miranda's desk and darted through the door ahead of him.

"I can't till your grandmother gets back with the groceries," she said. "Wet and cross. Oh dear. It bodes no good. I'll go open a can for Luna, which is also a poor idea unless it's foie gras."

Miranda followed the cat down the stairs while Bren and Shadow toiled another two flights up to the tiny attic apartment of the Bulgarian ex-opera star. She was practicing again, and this time her efforts were directed toward some goal in the upper register. Bren winced and Shadow whimpered as she began hopefully on a low note, climbed uncertainly through the middle range, and ended in an appalling, inhuman shriek.

On the top landing Bren knocked hastily before the singer could begin again. After a moment an eye appeared in the peephole in the door and then withdrew. This was followed by the sound of many bolts being shot and keys being turned. A dramatic pause then preceded the actual opening of the door, which was sudden and alarming. There was a cry of joy, and Bren found himself enveloped in the arms of the ancient soprano. Shadow, crouching on the threshold, began to bark.

"Bren! How joyful it is you have come! We will celebrate, but not, I think, your big friend," said Madame, closing the door firmly in Shadow's face.

"What are we celebrating, Madame Lavatky?" Bren asked. "I actually only came to see if I could borrow a book."

The singer released him and whirled away toward her

little alcove kitchen. She returned, flourishing a bottle of something that looked dark, viscous, and highly alcoholic.

"We celebrate the high C," she cried. "Three years I am working to find again my high C after my breakdown. You know I have terrible breakdown of the nerves, Bren? After the prison and the torture and so many things you are too young to hear."

Bren nodded, hoping he would not have to hear again any of the lurid and, so far as anyone could tell, totally imaginary incidents out of the opera singer's past. He was relieved to see that Madame Lavatky had not yet produced any glasses. Perhaps merely holding the bottle of villainous-looking liquid would be sufficiently festive.

"So," she went on triumphantly, "today I am achieving at last the very apex of my voice, the great high note which ends so many magnificent arias. You want to hear? The voice should rest, but for you, I sing it one more time."

"No, no, please," Bren protested. "I heard it perfectly coming up the stairs. It was beautiful, Madame Lavatky. Congratulations."

"We will drink, then," she said, swerving toward a cupboard full of glasses. "We will drink to my career — to my audition which I will have in only a few weeks at the Metropolitan Opera."

She carried bottle and glasses to a coffee table in one corner of the room, and Bren followed, drawn by the sight of a long bookcase of oversized books.

The soprano settled her ample form on the couch. Somewhere between sixty and eighty years old, she was still imposing but far from lovely, with her hair dyed shoe-polish black and her sagging features vividly made up. Bren accepted his sticky libation politely and raised the mercifully small glass to his mad hostess. "To your career, Madame Lavatky!" he cried and took a cautious sip. It was worse than he could possibly have imagined.

"To music, to art, to love!" she replied and tossed hers down.

Bren put his glass on the table, hoping he had done his duty by it, and twisted to look at the books behind his back. They seemed to be mostly in foreign languages, but one said something about the Ballet Russe. "I was hoping you had some books about ballet," he said. "Could I borrow one just for tonight? I have to write something for a class in school."

"Certainly, my dear young man," she said. "But why not study them here? So many are in French or Russian or Bulgarian. I could translate for you." Her eyes had grown moist after the toast, and she leaned her great bosom alarmingly close to Bren.

"I can read French," he said recklessly, "and I haven't had supper or taken Shadow out, so if you wouldn't mind. Just this one about the ballet russ would be fine." He gazed pleadingly at the singer, and she made an expansive gesture.

"Take it, take it. I do not need. And when you return, we will drink another little glass and maybe I sing for you or give you a tiny lesson in the French pronunciation. Yes?"

"That would be great, Madame Lavatky. Thanks a million," said Bren, and made hastily for the door, the heavy book clutched to his chest.

Bren got drenched walking Shadow, who dragged him from one dripping tree to another. He was tired and hungry, and the magical time he had spent with the slender girl in the theater seemed at least a hundred years ago.

Supper did nothing to lift his spirits. His grandmother, after wandering with increasing gloom from one sumptuous West Side food emporium to another, had finally come home empty-handed. What she thought she could afford, she didn't like; what she liked, she thought she couldn't afford. They dined on wet scrambled eggs and three-day-old corn muffins.

Alone at last in his room, Bren sprawled on his bed with the book while Shadow, curled by the radiator, snoozed and steamed a miasma of wet dogginess. Bren gazed dubiously at sepia prints of Russian ballerinas improbably poised on the tips of their toes. They wore white tutus and had abundant dark hair twisted severely at the napes of their incredibly long necks. They resembled Erika about as much as a troupe of ladies from Mars. Bren took a crack at the French, a language he had now studied for exactly ten days. To his surprise, some of it yielded to common sense, but large gaps remained.

"After all that trouble," he grumbled to his sleeping dog, "after having to be hugged and drink that foul stuff. I should have gone to the library and gotten out some idiot's delight — 'Everything you always wanted to know about ballet but were afraid to ask.' Now I'll still have to go to the library and take this stupid thing back besides."

Far away in the depths of the big house the phone rang, rang again, and was silent, followed by Miranda's voice calling. Bren slammed the book shut and galloped down the stairs. The phone was in the kitchen, but it had a long cord. When Bren heard the voice on the other end, he started backing toward the door to the hall, shaking and disentangling the cord as he went. The voice was husky and had a background suggestion of laughter. "Hey, Bren," it said. "I just had a thought."

"Does this happen often?" he countered, hoping he sounded reasonably cool and that she couldn't hear the pounding of his heart over the telephone. The cord was caught around the corner of a table. He gave it a savage wrench, which happily did not break the connection, and backed out the door.

"What about black light?" Erika said.

Bren thought fast but without coming up with an answer. "What about it?" he asked. "Elaborate, please. Throw just a few more words around."

"For the witches, Bren. We could wear body paint that only shows in black light, and you could turn black light on us, and we would look really weird. I saw it in a disco once, and it was absolutely awesome."

"Hey, yeah. What a neat idea," Bren said. "I can see it now." He could, too, including a vision of Erika in body paint.

"The only problem is," she went on, "what about the other people?"

"What other people?"

"Macbeth and Banquo and whoever else actually sees the witches," Erika answered with just a trace of impatience. "They would have to be standing around in the dark. I can just see the great Brian Rushmore's face when he finds that we have all that lovely light and he has none. But of course it wouldn't work," she added regretfully. "They have to be lit."

"Is Brian Macbeth?" Bren asked.

"My dear, he is not only Macbeth. He is every single important role that has been played at the Perkins School in the last three years, or so I've been told. Where have you been?"

"In the park, mostly," Bren said, and Erika gave her enticing chuckle. She thinks I'm kidding, he thought.

"Anyway, brood about it," she said. "See if you can think of a way to get around that little problem of the other actors wanting to be seen."

"I will," Bren promised, "and I'll ask Eli. He's much more technical than I am."

"Terrific. See you tomorrow, Bren," she said, and hung up before he had a chance to think of a good last line.

The evening had taken a definite turn for the better, Bren felt, as he put the phone back in its niche. He started for the door again, ignoring the feverish gleam of curiosity in his mother's eyes, but stopped in his tracks as she remarked, seemingly at random, "What a pity it's going to rain all weekend. The extended forecast is really grisly, and pushing back a major front is much more work than I have time for at the moment."

Bren had never been confident of his mother's ability to change the weather, and he was also reasonably sure that she was teasing him. Now, however, was no time to take chances with the supernatural. He turned and fixed Miranda with a look that was scarcely less penetrating than her own. "That will be awful," he said, "but I think there's a rain date for the dance program, and it will be fine weather for frogs. Maybe you can catch some in the park as they come out to enjoy the downpour."

"What a mean thing to say!" Miranda cried, apparently forgetting that she was responsible for this unkindness.

"It wasn't meant to be," Bren said. "I didn't say you had to chase frogs through the rain, dear old Mom. I only said if you did, it would probably be a good time for it. Good night, all." And he left for his room feeling reasonably pleased with the exchange.

Chapter Five

Bren woke to an ambiguous dawn and walked to school under a brightening sky, but across the Hudson the shore of New Jersey still crouched under a line of black clouds. Off there in the west, where New York weather was made, the battle was still undecided. This being Thursday, only two days before the dance program (for which there was no rain date), it seemed late to adopt a wait-and-see policy. Bren stopped before the entrance to the Perkins School and considered the kidnaping of a small but lively animal from one of its overcrowded rooms. After a bit he shrugged and went on in. He had all day to worry and reconnoiter.

At lunchtime he climbed to the fourth floor and peered through the glass panel of the door to the biology lab. Mrs. Packard was seated at her desk before a mountain of exam papers. She was the only teacher who had even thought of giving a test during the first week of school. Now she would probably stay late to grade them. Bren craned his neck trying to see the frog tank, which was just out of his line of vision. Suppose it was empty; then all this mental anguish would have been for nothing. Bren squared his shoulders and opened the door. He walked briskly to the frog tank, observed that it was teeming with life, and turned to meet the gimlet eye of Mrs. Packard.

"Young man, were you looking for something?" she said.

"A friend," Bren answered hurriedly. "I was looking for a friend in your class, but he's not here."

"Not among the frogs?" Mrs. Packard asked. From any other teacher this would have been a joke, but Bren felt that levity was not intended and would be ill advised in return.

"Not anywhere that I can see," he said. "But thank you anyway, Mrs. Packard. Good-bye."

He closed the door to the biology room and wandered down the stairs, pondering his problem. So much depended, finally, on the presence or absence of Mrs. Packard after school that he decided to put it out of his mind and look for Erika. The school, though small, was full of odd corners where students at noon were eating sandwiches, reading books, or talking. An exhaustive search of the high school building, however, failed to turn up Erika and used the remainder of Bren's lunch hour, nor was she in physics, which was the only class they had in common.

Hungry and discouraged, Bren tried to apply himself to the laws of acceleration. This was a subject dear to the heart of Edward Bear, who, in the interest of making the abstract concrete, had set up a sloping wooden chute running the entire length of the classroom. The extreme gentleness of the incline permitted Mr. Behrens to run to the bottom and catch the rapidly accelerating little ball that he had started at the top. This he did several times to the delight (if not, perhaps, the enlightenment) of his class. Bren felt more cheerful as he watched — frogs and the inexplicable absence of Erika forgotten during his favorite teacher's enthusiastic performance.

Erika got back to school only in time for the last two classes of the day and would not have bothered to come at all but for the hope of seeing the brown-haired boy with the meltingly open smile. "Relentlessly normal" was the way she described Bren to herself, wondering at the same time why this should appeal to her usually more exotic tastes. She also wanted sympathy and had not yet made any close friends to listen to her complaints. For Erika had not only missed a diverting physics class, she had acquired a large, prickly mouthful of braces on her nearly perfect teeth. "Nobody's going to want to kiss me for a few years, that's for sure," she muttered to herself as she climbed the steps to the school. "Might as well cuddle up with a barbed wire fence."

The last two classes were boring, like the day itself, which continued to be overcast, and Erika felt her spirits sink slowly through the plodding lectures like a waterlogged leaf in a stagnant pond. Finally the last hour dragged to an end, and she was free to search for Bren. A more patient person would have waited by the door, but Erika was not patient. She thought his last class was on the top floor next to the biology lab, so she began to climb against the descending stream of students, pausing at each floor to look up and down the hall. On three she was stopped by Mr. Behrens, who wanted to deplore the fact that she had missed his performance. "And now you'll never understand acceleration, poor girl," he finished. "There's no return engagement or even an encore."

"This is devastating," Erika said. "Whatever shall I do?" It was hard to be sprightly without opening her mouth more

44

than an eighth of an inch, and this she had resolved not to do.

"You could read the book," Mr. Behrens countered, "but the movie's more exciting. What's the matter with your mouth?"

Erika bared her teeth for the first time in a ferocious smile.

"Blindingly beautiful," said Edward Bear. "I hope you don't bite."

Fond as she was of her physics teacher, Erika was beginning to worry that Bren might escape by some means other than the only stairway. "Just people who stand between me and the girls' room," she said and, squeezing past him, ran up the last flight of stairs to the fourth floor.

Bren was not in the economics room, and there was only one more place to look. Erika peered through the glass door of the biology lab. An arresting scene met her eyes.

The big, bare room appeared to teem with frogs, and through the frogs strode Bren in desperate haste, stooping and snatching at the elusive throng. Erika stared and then began to laugh. She opened the door, and Bren turned, a gleam of manic fury in his eye.

"Shut that door, idiot!" he shouted, then stopped, one hand clutching a struggling frog, the other his already disordered hair, as he saw who it was. "Oh, my God. You of all people," he said. "What have I done to deserve this?"

"What have you done, period?" Erika asked. "Do you need, maybe, some sort of help?"

"Do I need help? What does it look like I need? Help me put these unspeakable creatures back where they came from. I had no idea they could move so fast." Bren waded cautiously over to the frog tank with his victim.

Erika had managed to grasp the situation, if not the reason for it. She held the lid of the tank while Bren popped the first frog in and hastily closed it again.

"That's good," he said. "This is definitely a two-man job. I could be here all night, and if Mrs. Packard comes back . . ." He rolled his eyes to heaven and went back to catching frogs. Between the two of them, the work went fairly fast. Erika, having less to do, watched with fascination. Nor did she miss the final act when Bren, turning his back to her at the farthest corner of the room, stuffed the last frog down the front of his shirt and buttoned it up to his throat. Wisely, she decided to say nothing about this curious sight.

"Whew! What a relief. Thanks a million, Erika. I couldn't have done it by myself." Bren's smile was almost back to normal, and the small, wiggling bulge just above his belt would not have been noticed by the casual observer.

"Now are you going to tell me what this was all in aid of?" Erika asked.

"Not until we get out of here," Bren said. "Come on, let's split before the dragon lady comes back. I'll walk you home," he added. It seemed the least he could do, though what he was going to say once they were safely out of the biology lab was at the moment beyond even his powers of invention.

"Great, let's go," she said, and giving one last glance at the tank of hysterical frogs, they left. Mrs. Packard was toiling up the stairs as they came down, a stack of exam papers clutched to her bony chest, a look of generalized suspicion in her cold, blue eyes. "She's going to wonder why her charges are so upset," Bren said, "but what the hey, she'll never guess."

Erika giggled. "Unless we forgot one," she said. "I could swear I saw one last frog hopping away toward the corner of the room."

"You were seeing things," Bren said firmly.

"Let's hope so," Erika said, and treated him to the full splendor of her smile.

They had now reached the sidewalk, and Bren stopped to look at her carefully for the first time. He saw a wonderful diversion from the subject of frogs — the spectacular mouthful of hardware that Erika had forgotten she had.

"That's an amazing set of braces," he said. "When did you get those? I mean, you can't have had them all along."

Erika clamped her mouth shut. "Thishafternoon," she mumbled.

"What? Today? That's why I couldn't find you at lunchtime." She nodded mutely. "But you've got to talk," he went on. "You can't go through life with your mouth shut."

"Wanna bet?" Erika said, only a little more distinctly.

"You were talking in the bio room," Bren said. "Come on. Open up. Lots of beautiful women have braces, though I didn't think there was anything wrong with your teeth before."

This comment was enough to pry open Erika's jaws. "You're damn right there was nothing wrong with my teeth," she cried. "But everybody's got to have an expensive orthodontist, didn't you know? So I've got to have one too. Daddy ran out of nice things to give me, so he gave me these."

This was news from another world to Bren, who stood at a loss for words, looking at the furious girl. Suddenly the front of his shirt gave a convulsive jump and Erika's eyes widened.

She had forgotten for the moment a subject of even more absorbing interest than her teeth.

"But let's not talk about me," she said, her eyes fixed on Bren's middle. "I think frogs are a much more interesting topic of conversation, and I want to know *all* about them."

"Of course you do," Bren said. He was playing for time while his mind scrambled after explanations, each one more improbable than the last, for the ridiculous scene in the bio lab. "I mean, naturally, after finding me like that, more or less knee-deep in frogs. Anyone would wonder."

"Anyone would, and I do," Erika said.

"It's a statistical project," Bren said in a rush. "For math. You know how practical Miss Wentworth is, or don't you? I forget you weren't here last year. It's part of the new math, I think. Like, no more meaningless theorems. No more dry examples. Everything must be related to life."

Erika nodded gravely. "I can see the life part all right," she said, "but the mathematics still eludes me."

"Statistics," Bren said. "I thought I'd count their spots and do a correlation."

Math was, unfortunately, one of Erika's strong points. "A correlation with what?" she asked.

Lacking a ready answer to this, Bren plunged on. "Anyway, you can imagine how impossible it was to count the spots on a bunch of frogs all hopping around in a tank and getting on top of each other, so I saw there was an empty tank in the corner and thought I'd take them one by one, count, put them in the other tank, then dump the whole lot back. But things got out of hand," he finished with a helpless gesture that made Erika laugh.

48

"You're really crazy," she said. "I like that."

"You do?" Bren asked dubiously.

"Absolutely. I hate ordinary, predictable people. Come on, let's walk. I've got to get home and see if I can eat. Ugh! What a thing to look forward to."

"You could take nourishment through a straw," Bren suggested.

"For two years?"

"That's true. You'd fade away."

"You can't be too thin or too rich," Erika said, "but I think it would sap my strength and ruin my temper. What a marvelous afternoon."

Bren nodded happily. They were walking up toward Broadway with the late sun shining warmly on their backs. "It's turning nice for Saturday," he said, adding to himself, "if I can only keep this damn frog alive."

Turning right on Broadway, they passed the seductive windows of Zabar's — "No, I really can't give up eating," Erika said. As they crossed Seventy-ninth Street, the river flashed blue at the bottom of the hill, and the rusticated stone of Erika's building rose into view like a fortress.

Bren stopped at the tall gates and looked in at the fountains playing in the shadowy courtyard. "I always wanted to know someone who lived here," he said. "What a neat place."

"Come on up," Erika said. "You can help me choose something to eat and then look the other way while I savage it."

Bren was tempted, but only for a moment. The scrabbling sensation around his middle was growing weaker, and he wasn't sure whether his mother would be pleased with a dead offering. There was also the strong probability that a more relaxed, indoor conversation with Erika would again turn toward treacherous waters. "I can't this time," he said. "There's something I've really got to do."

"Okay. 'Bye for now," Erika said, and turned in through the gate.

As Bren started back up Broadway, he could hear the doorman's cheerful voice, "Hey, Erika, what'd you do? Swallow a box of paper clips?" There was no reply.

Chapter Six

The sky darkened again as Bren crossed Broadway and walked toward the park. Huge clouds were rising as if from some infernal cauldron in New Jersey, and the last rays of sun crept between them, casting a lurid glow on all that only a few moments ago had basked in the light of a clear September afternoon.

Bren felt his spirits sink with the failing light. He wanted to hurry now — to get home and rid himself of his increasingly unpleasant burden — but his footsteps dragged as he trudged the last block to his house.

Curiously, in view of his upbringing, or perhaps because of it, Bren was not given to brooding or to superstition. Now, however, he felt the ebbing life of the miserable creature inside his shirt as if it were his own. For the first time, he found himself thinking about the actual fate of a frog at the hands of a witch — a witch who also happened to be his mother.

Erika, he reflected bitterly, might prefer people who were out of the ordinary, but the eccentricities of Miranda West went beyond the merely unconventional. He wondered if one could have a lasting relationship with a girl and never bring her home. Many teenagers seemed to be ashamed of their parents and their living quarters, but this notion was foreign to Bren. He had always felt close to his mother and fortunate to live with her in the extraordinary old house. Now it occurred to him that he would do well to invent some dreary setting for his home life — a tiny, cramped apartment in one of the tenements that stood between Broadway and the park. It was an unappealing idea and one which would probably prove difficult to sustain.

The gray stone house looked forbidding in the darkening afternoon. No lights shone from the long, narrow windows; it had an expectant air, as if it waited for some shattering event — a scream, a bolt of lightning, a dark figure hurtling from its topmost floor. Bren was surprised to find his home so suddenly transformed into the set for a low-budget horror movie. "Halloween," he muttered, as he climbed the stairs. "It's being a Halloween house, and this is Halloween weather."

He slammed the front door and headed for his mother's studio, a strangely subdued Shadow slinking at his heels. The stairwell was filled with an eerie glow as light filtered through the stained glass skylight. From above floated Madame Lavatky's scales, making the silence below seem more intense.

"Enough of this," Bren said, and started flipping light switches as he went. He unbuttoned his shirt and dropped the frog into the terrarium, where, to his relief, it opened its eyes and limped bravely off to the pool.

The house had seemed empty when he came in, but his grandmother appeared from the shadowy depths of the parlor as he went down the stairs. "So here's the young prince," she cried. "Every light in the house he must have on, but does he pay the electric bill? Not he!"

"I'll get a paper route," Bren said, "and give my all to old

Con Ed, but please, Gram, let's have some light. It's such a gruesome afternoon."

Rose stopped with her hand on the light switch. "Got the willies, have you? Me too. Something's brewing today for sure. Get your mother away from that black witch is what I say, or creepy will come to crawly, and what goes bump in the night might come to stay."

Bren was now genuinely alarmed. "They're down there together?" he asked. "*Doing* things, you mean?"

Rose nodded. "They're down there together," she said, "and if you think they're knitting baby clothes, you're entitled to your opinion."

"I'll take a look," said Bren, resolute now, the man of the house. He was not, in fact, afraid of either his mother or Louise LaReine, having lived with both of them all his life, but he very much disliked the idea of their combining forces. "Shadow, you stay here," he added as he started down the basement stairs. Shadow, in fact, showed no enthusiasm for a merry chase among black chickens. He lay down at the head of the stairs and followed Bren's descent with worried brown eyes, a whimper at the back of his throat, the plume of his tail quiet on the floor.

The door was ajar, and Bren gave it a gentle push. It opened onto a surprisingly large, low-ceilinged room which was painted black and hung with dark purple draperies. At the farthest end a black table stood inside a white triangle painted on the floor. There was a cupboard full of dusty bottles behind the table, and on it a thurible which sent a column of smoke wavering up around a small brass pot suspended by three chains. Here, in the cozy glow of a fringed Victorian lamp, Bren saw the two witches. They were not knitting baby booties, it was true, but neither were they summoning dark winds or ghastly spirits of the deep. Miranda and Louise appeared to be cooking and exchanging recipes.

Louise chose a bottle and shook something tiny into the palm of her hand. "Eye of newt," she said. "Can't seem to make anything without old eye of newt."

"I know," Miranda said, "but they're so hard to cut up, and a whole one always seems to be too much."

"Just make a lot and put it on the shelf. This stuff don't spoil, babe. It can't spoil. No way. Not if you put it through the flame and say the words." Louise popped the newt's eye into the pot, and Miranda leaned over to sniff the steam.

"Evil," she said, drawing back. "It smells awful, Louise. Nobody's going to drink that stuff voluntarily."

Louise shook her head. "Miranda, child, how many times I have to explain? First the things of power you put in and make sure they be well charmed up, then the sweet things of field and woods to make it good. Now rhino horn."

"We shouldn't, you know," protested Miranda. "The poor rhinos are almost extinct just because of people like us."

Louise put down the jar she was holding with a thump. "You think you charm a man without rhino horn? You just show me how. Go on. Find something." She gestured at the row of bottles. "I truly waiting to be surprised."

"Well, maybe just a pinch," Miranda said. "You're right; there just is no substitute, and after all, this rhino perished long ago. There's no point letting it go to waste. I don't expect to be needing this particular potion again."

Louise snorted. "Better make it strong, then," she said, shaking the gray powder into the pot. "You won't hook that cold fish with any wimpy little pinch of horn."

"It's not me he doesn't like," Miranda explained. "It's everything else." She sniffed again. "Mmmm. Better already. I wonder how this will taste with Scotch?"

Bren had listened shamelessly from his dark vantage point near the door. Now he felt that he had heard enough. He cleared his throat and advanced into the room. "Do you know what time it is?" he said. "Couldn't we think about cooking something a little more nourishing?"

Miranda gave a guilty start. "Oh, Bren, is school over? I completely lost track."

"School has been over for a century," Bren said, "and the house is so gloomy even Gram's got the creeps. Come up and make like a mother for a while, if it's not asking too much."

Miranda turned back to her crony. "Louise, dear, can you wind up the charm by yourself? You're so much better at it than I am, and duty calls."

"You better believe I am, babe," Louise said. "I just surprised you trust me alone with your potion. How you know I won't turn your fish into a goat?"

Louise chuckled at her own humor, and Miranda fixed her with a bright, blue stare. "Oh, I'm not worried about that," she said. "As a certain fish once pointed out, the price of real estate on the West Side has gone much too high in the last few years for anyone to take any chances. But thanks, Lou, for all the help and for the rhino horn. I'll pay you back for that."

Miranda blew a kiss to her sister witch and followed Bren up the stairs. When they reached the hall, Bren said, "I got your wretched frog, by the way, which is why I'm late, so if you're fiddling with the weather, you can stop."

"Oh, Bren, that is good news," his mother said. "But I

wasn't, you know — fiddling with the weather, as you put it. All of this changing from clouds to sun and back again is someone else's work entirely." Miranda cast a pious glance in the direction of the skylight, then turned back to look closely at Bren. "How long were you down there watching us?" she asked.

"Not long, but long enough," Bren said. "If you think you're going to mix that glop with twelve-year-old whisky and get an expert like Dad to drink it, you must be crazy. You couldn't fob that stuff off on a Bowery bum."

"Oh dear, I hope you're wrong," Miranda said. "I thought we could invent a new cocktail or something."

"Lots of luck," said Bren. "Just lots and lots of luck, Mom."

The kitchen was nearly dark except for the fire and the light from the refrigerator, into which Rose peered with wrinkled nose. "Leftover brussels sprouts," she said. "Turnips, cabbage, and something that might be last week's spaghetti with clam sauce."

"Steaks in the freezer," Miranda countered. "The kind you can thaw in no time — baby peas and French fried potatoes."

Bren laughed and turned on the lights, suddenly feeling better than he had all day. "Take your choice," he said, "but I'm with Mom. This is definitely a steak and French fries night."

"Food to banish the supernatural?" Miranda asked with a knowing smile. "Well, we can try. Get a potato peeler, Bren, and we'll whip up a hearty, all-American meal."

Chapter Seven

Bren woke Saturday to see the leaves of the maple outside his window drenched with a light of such purity and grace that he seemed to be looking out on the first morning of creation. He knew that he would spend not only the evening, but the entire day in Central Park, first with his father, then with his new love. What more could one ask of life? He stretched, feeling the inner contentment of one who has suffered much to arrive at a just reward. The days of rain and of what still seemed like rather unrewarding drudgery for Eli, the traumatic afternoon of the frogs — all, Bren felt, had brought him this perfect Saturday.

After a hasty breakfast, he snapped on Shadow's leash and headed for the park. It was still early by his father's standards, but they had a favorite place, and Bren knew he could go there and be confident that Bob would turn up. From the entrance at Eighty-first Street he turned north on a winding, hilly path and came at last to the quiet shores of the small lake near 103rd Street. Here he slipped off Shadow's leash and watched the big dog gallop along the shore and finally dash into the water up to his chest. There were weeping willows on the margins of the lake, their green cascades now laced with chains of gold. Each tree had been a castle to Bren when he was small. Now he found a short stick and stood under a shimmering canopy to throw it again and again for Shadow until his father arrived.

Bob West came jogging in white shorts and a red shirt with an alligator on the pocket. He was carrying a large bag full of things that could be thrown and caught.

"Hey, Bren," he said, panting to a halt under the willow tree and dumping his bag on the ground.

"Hey, Dad. How's it going? Down, Shadow, you ass!"

"Not bad. How about this weather? What did you do to deserve this?"

"Plenty," Bren said, "but let's not talk about that."

"I brought a batch of stuff to throw," his father said proudly, pointing at the bag.

Bren picked up a football and ran with it across the green field that sloped up from the lake. He threw it hard, and Bob caught it on the run and threw it back. They did this for some time to the frustration of Shadow, who ran back and forth under the ball and never managed to get his teeth into it.

"You're getting good at this," Bob commented when they paused for breath. "Too bad you'll never play the rest of the game. Even if they have it wherever you go to college, it'll be much too late to start."

"That's all right," Bren said. "Believe it or not, Dad, I can live the rest of my life without having some giant knock me down in the mud and step on my face."

"You've actually got a point," his father admitted. "I never cared for it myself."

Bren laughed. "Then why be sorry that I'm missing all that ghastly fun?"

"I don't know. It seemed like a proper, fatherly sentiment."

"You're weird. Let's play something Shadow can play. He'll never be a football player either, although he might make a good tackle. Let's play three-cornered Frisbee."

"You know the weakness of that idea," Bob said, fishing the Frisbee out of the bag.

"Yeah, I know. Shadow can't throw," Bren said, "but he deserves a break. Come on."

They spent the rest of the morning throwing and catching things. Bren thought it was one of the better mornings of his life.

In the early afternoon they wandered south to the shores of another lake in a part of the park where there was more to eat and drink. It had grown quite hot. Bob bought hot dogs and Cokes, and they flopped in the shade by the water.

"So how's your mother and all the other strange ladies?" Bob asked, after a period of peaceful munching.

"Mom's fine," Bren said, and paused. He really didn't want the conversation that now seemed inevitable. "They're all fine," he added reluctantly. "They're a lot like they were when you saw them last except Madame Lavatky, who is happier, I think. She reached high C, or so she says. Nice for her, but a bit hard on the rest of us."

"Your mother is a saint to put up with that screeching," Bob said, and then laughed. "That's a good one. Miranda the saint. I never thought of her in quite that way before."

"She may not be a saint," Bren said. "Who wants a saint for a mother anyway? But she does put up with a lot, and it's a big house. Full of women," he added bitterly.

"That's subtle, Bren," his father said.

"It wasn't meant to be. Come on, Dad. I can't believe you really like living in that beehive all by yourself."

"When I could have such stimulating company in the House of Usher?" Bob asked. "You'd better believe I do."

Bren was silent, staring out across the lake, thinking that his perfect day was taking a turn for the worse. Finally he muttered, "Well, I want you to come back, and so does Mom, in case you hadn't noticed, but I guess you couldn't care less."

"Look, Bren," his father said, "I love your mother, okay? Got that?" Bren nodded gloomily. "But she just doesn't keep a tight enough ship for me. I can't get up in the morning and find a baby bat in my shoe — one of my Gucci shoes — and then find that someone's been monkeying with my shaving cream. My whole face turned green, for Christ's sake, at seven o'clock in the morning." The ghost of a smile appeared on Bren's face and was quickly suppressed. "You think that's funny. You should try it sometime when you're going to breakfast with four top executives."

"It must have been awful," Bren said.

"Awful doesn't begin to describe it. Childish. Maddening. But if that kind of thing only happened once in a while, I could put up with it. I *have* put up with it. Sixteen years I put up with a house full of weird smells and weird sounds and creepy animals turning up in unexpected places. Do you know what I found in my shirt drawer the day I left my hearth and home for good?" Bren nodded, but Bob paid no attention. "A goddamned python," he said. "That's what I found. It makes for marital wear and tear, Bren. I can't put it any more plainly than that."

"I think she might try to be more considerate," Bren said, "if — you know . . ." He let the sentence trail away.

"She might," Bob conceded. "But even if she reformed, there'd still be the grim old lady with the crystal ball, the squalling of the mad Bulgarian, lovely Louise, and loathsome Luna."

Bren took the last swallow of his Coke and tossed the can into the trash basket. "I guess I understand," he said. "At least a bit better than I used to. I'm looking forward to some similar troubles myself, as a matter of fact."

"You are? How come? I thought you were all adjusted to the madhouse. You ought to be by now."

"Yeah, well, it's a question of having friends to the house," Bren said. "You can imagine."

"Can I ever," Bob said, and then with growing comprehension, "Oh, Lord, girlfriends! You poor kid. You really could have a problem there."

"Let your imagination roam," Bren said. "Conjure up a few pictures of what could happen. That's what I've been doing, and each new scenario is more gruesome than the last."

"You've met someone?" his father asked cautiously. "Someone you would theoretically like to bring home?"

"It's not so much that I'd like to bring her home," Bren explained. "It's that I don't see any way out of it. She's hopelessly curious, which is one of the things that makes her so neat, and we live so close to each other. Apart from telling her the whole house is infected with smallpox, I really can't think of an excuse."

"I'll put my mind to the problem," Bob promised. "After

all, it's not as if I lack experience. Young executives with large houses are expected to entertain. Remember the time those two senior vice presidents and their wives came to dinner?"

Bren shook his head. "I was at camp, but I heard rumors when I came home."

"Your mother, to be fair, tried quite hard," Bob went on, "and looked absolutely gorgeous. We cleared out the fortune-telling stuff, and Rose actually stuck to her cooking and did one of her better things, grumbling and casting black looks, but nothing beyond what a slightly eccentric old lady might do. Luna was locked in the studio. The salamander was evicted from the bathtub. Madame was persuaded not to practice for one night. The only uncontrollable factor was Louise, and of course, where there's a weak link in a chain, that's where it's going to snap."

"You can't influence Louise," Bren said. "She's a force of nature." He had heard this story before, but never from his father's point of view.

Bob proceeded with gloomy relish. "All went well until we were gathered in the living room for coffee — all nice and genteel and boring as hell, I have to admit, but still, just the way I wanted it to be. Then the door bangs open and there's our friend in full fig — purple dashiki, orange turban all covered with those funny signs. To make it worse, she decides to go into an Aunt Jemima routine: 'Oh, Missy West. Ah sho' is sorry. If Ah'd knowed you all had company, Ah nevah would come in like this.' Your mother now makes a fatal mistake and puts on her gracious monarch turn: 'Never mind, Louise, dear,' she says, 'but perhaps whatever it was could wait?' 'Wait it cannot,' cries Louise — the black queen challenging the white queen. 'The spell be wound, the fire burns, the twin smokes rise, and not a pinch of henbane do I have. But don't you stir, my lady. Just give me the key to your cupboard, and I'll fetch it myself.' 'You'll do nothing of the sort,' your mother says and marches dear Louise right out the door. Unfortunately, the damage had been done, and when there was an opening farther up in the company, those two VPs were strangely reluctant to consider me."

"Awful," Bren said, "but still, only money and a job. I've got a girl, or at least I think I do."

His father laughed and scrambled to his feet. "Play it by ear, Bren," he said. "Just play it by ear, old son. That's what I always had to do."

Chapter Eight

Alone in the big apartment she shared with her father, Erika sat on the covered radiator in the living room window and watched the sun set over the Hudson. It had been a long day with nothing to do but look forward to the evening. Now, almost against her will, she thought about Bren. It's too soon, she told herself sternly. I hardly know him. All we're going to do is have a neat date, see something I want to see on a fall evening in New York. But in a different part of her mind she already knew that Bren was not just another boy. There had been plenty of those in Philadelphia, where she had lived the stormy, miserable years of her early teens. She smoothed the fur of the plush baby seal she held in her lap, her last stuffed animal, the one she was never going to give up. "Well, Silky, he certainly couldn't be more different," she said. "Maybe he's someone even Dad would approve of, that is, if he's got pots of money along with good looks and good manners. Ugh. I can't believe this is happening to me."

What seemed to Erika to be a long procession of boyfriends filed past in her imagination — older boys mostly, good dancers with cars who took her places she wasn't allowed to go, handsome, fun-loving, and ultimately disappointing. "I'm getting old, I'm settling down!" she said to the stuffed seal. "What a funny thing to happen in New York, of all places."

Erika stared at the red ball of the sun, willing it to set, and because it was already so close to the horizon, it seemed to obey her command. Briefly the shore of New Jersey, with its isolated towers, was silhouetted against an orange sky. The river was dark blue watered silk, on which a single white sail skimmed in to harbor at the Seventy-ninth Street boat basin.

Erika felt a growing sensation of warmth in her seat. The radiator was coming on. "It's going to be cold tonight," she said, and she jumped up and strode off to her bedroom for a serious consultation with her wardrobe.

The long closet was divided into two distinct collections, one (large) consisting of clothes her father had bought and she refused to wear, the other (small) of her own purchases. Ranks of tweed skirts with matching cashmere sweaters, of silk shirts, tailored slacks, and jersey dresses gave way to a row of more eccentric garments, predominantly black. Already dressed in black jeans and a white, ribbed turtleneck, Erika added a black V-neck sweater that was several sizes too large for her slender frame and stood back to study the effect in the full-length mirror. She pushed the sleeves of the sweater up to her elbows and added a huge, black digital watch to one white-clad wrist.

"Warm enough?" she asked the girl in the mirror. "Well, maybe not." She reflected that Bren, though clearly a passionate and creative person, might be a slow starter when it came to keeping a person warm, so she pulled out a black gypsy shawl tasseled with jet beads. "Mmmm, festive," Erika

65

murmured when she had layered the shawl over the sweater. She glanced at her outsized watch, saw that only fifteen minutes remained of the interminable day, and decided to meet Bren in the courtyard.

Bren approached the Apthorp with a quaking heart and cast about for an explanation to banish the tremors that grew with every step he took toward the tall iron gates. Neither his continuing ignorance of the ballet nor the forbidding aspect of Erika's building seemed enough to cause such turmoil. He refused to recognize his symptoms as the disorder known to all on the brink of an important first date.

The courtyard was filled with autumn dusk, warmed by the glow of the ornamental lamps around the garden and a scatter of lighted windows in the gray walls. It was very quiet. Bren could hear the splash of the fountains, and then he saw Erika by the nearest one, straining her eyes into the gloom. The light picked out her white turtleneck, her small white face and strawberry hair.

"Hey, Bren?" she called softly, as if still unsure who he was, and stood up as he crossed the driveway into the garden. They confronted each other, tongue-tied for a moment.

"What a spooky place," Bren said at last. "Doesn't anybody ever come or go?"

"This is just a weird, in-between sort of time," she said. "Half an hour ago the shrieking of five-year-olds and thunder of tricycles was probably deafening, and any minute now there'll be beautiful people popping out of all four doors headed for night life — just like us," she finished with a flashing silver smile.

"I see you've given up keeping your mouth shut," Bren said.

"The vow of silence was just too much. I felt like a cloistered nun."

"You don't look like a nun, cloistered or otherwise," Bren said with an admiring glance at her exotic wrappings. "Have you got enough on? I brought a blanket."

"Clever you. We'll bundle," Erika said. "Do you know what that is?"

"I think so," Bren said cautiously, and the uneasy, lurching sensations returned.

Erika laughed. "Come on, then, let's blow this genteel scene and head for the wilds of Central Park."

Walking with Erika was fun, if rather exhausting. She had a swift, long stride for someone so small, and plenty of breath left over for talk.

"I love New York," she said, gazing up and down Broadway as they waited for the light. "I'm sorry. I have to learn not to say that. I always think of a little red heart being dropped, plunk, right in the middle of my sentence, knocking out the 'love' and sticking in a sort of 'umph' in its place. Stupid."

"Well, it's good you umph New York, anyway," Bren said. "Where are you from?"

"Philadelphia. Such boredom you can't imagine, and we lived in a quiet neighborhood — not even a deli for miles. I took to playing hard-core at volume ten, you know? So the neighbors went up in arms, and Dad threatened to send me away to school, and I said, please do, but nothing came of it except a little temporary excitement. This place is heaven, believe me."

"I do," Bren said. "But when you're here for a while, you start looking for quiet places — like the park. But maybe that's not your thing — trees and grass and open spaces."

"Oh, it is!" Erika said. "It's just respectability I hate. Where do you live?"

"Over there," Bren said, with a vague gesture to the north. "In a house, but it's not very respectable. I mean it's a nice house, but — oh, a little . . . bizarre," he finished, wondering why, out of his large vocabulary, he had not been able to dredge up a less intriguing word.

"Bizarre?" Erika said. "How nice. I'll visit you. Do you have what's known as an intact family? That always sounds so sort of frozen. Mom and Dad grinning by the car. Boy and girl romping with dog."

"Not exactly," Bren said. "Except for the dog, who does romp quite a lot, but only with me. No sister, and my parents are separated. I live with my mother and grandmother and assorted tenants — all female."

"Nobody stays married anymore," she said. "It's such a drag."

"My parents might get back together," Bren said. "They seem to want to, but they drive each other crazy. Dad comes to dinner at least once a week, and they make a lot of jokes and flirt with each other, and then he goes home."

"Don't complain," Erika said. They were waiting for the light at Central Park West. Beyond the stream of traffic loomed the dark trees of the park. Bren examined the small face at his shoulder and thought for a moment that it looked immensely sad. "Mom went galloping off to fulfill herself as a woman about ten years ago," she went on, "and hasn't been heard from since. But it's not so bad," she added, seeing the look on Bren's face. "A person gets a lot of freedom living

68

with a father — especially a busy, rich father. You get everything you want and the time to enjoy it."

"Including braces on your teeth?" Bren asked.

"Well, he ran out of ideas temporarily. There have been
other, compensating goodies." (Like a closet full of clothes I
never wear, she thought, but the smile she turned on Bren
was full of impish glee.)

They crossed into the park and followed the wide, lighted
path toward the theater.

"I used to come here every day when I was a little kid,"
Bren said, pointing to the playground on their left. "Eli and
I would come with one of our mothers or Louise LaReine.
She's a ferocious black woman who lives in our basement
apartment and does a few things for Mom instead of paying
rent."

"What a marvelous name," Erika said. "It sounds more
romantic than ferocious. What did she do, spank you when
your parents were out? We had a maid who did that — only
once, I must admit."

"Nothing like that." Bren felt suddenly comfortable with
the subject of Louise, as if he could load all the peculiarities
of his household onto her broad personality. "Louise is a
voodoo woman. She casts spells and goes about muttering
dark threats."

"That sounds delicious, but a funny choice for a nurse-
maid."

"Oh, Louise is harmless once you get used to her, and
I've known her all my life. Besides, my mother is . . ." Bren
found himself again at a loss for the right word.

"Broad-minded?" Erika suggested.

"That's it. Broad-minded, and not easy to scare the way most mothers are. Eli's mother used to have a fit when Louise took us to the park, but she couldn't resist the temptation to get out of doing it herself. She's a psychologist, and she thought Louise was going to give us all kinds of nightmares and complexes."

"And did she?"

"Not that I've noticed," Bren said cheerfully.

They crossed the road that cut through the park below the Delacorte Theater and climbed the short hill. Now comes the hard part, Bren thought, as they settled into their seats in the rapidly filling outdoor auditorium.

It turned out that there was no need for learned comments on the art of the dance. Erika was in her element. She gazed happily at the great, semicircular sweep of the stage and the tall lighting towers. "What a beautiful theater," she said. "You're so lucky to have grown up close to it."

Bren, whose visits to the Delacorte had been few, still managed to dredge up some memories from summers past. "I hope they'll light the castle," he said, pointing off into the dark. "The Central Park weather station is up there on the cliff across the lake in that imitation castle, so sometimes they light it up for a backdrop."

"Fabulous. I can't wait." Erika wriggled contentedly in her seat, and Bren wondered if she was getting cold. The temperature was certainly dropping as they waited for the ballet to begin, and the blanket still lay rolled in his lap — like a time bomb, he thought, casting a nervous glance at the girl beside him.

Now, slowly, the bleak floodlights faded to darkness, and for a moment they could see a scatter of stars over the dim bulk of the castle. From somewhere a thin, wild melody began to grow — strange and elusive, as if from the void behind the stars.

Then a bright passageway appeared between the trees, and down this corridor of light came three young men at furious speed. They were nearly naked, their bodies sashed with streamers of red cloth. Through the trees and onto the bare stage they came, running and whirling, savage, demonic, as the music rose. Bren felt the hair rise on the back of his neck and forgot to think about what he was seeing. There was no story, or if there was, it was one his bones and blood had known before he was born — one his ancestors had known in the firelight that pushed back the dark at the mouth of the cave.

The music dropped, and he held his breath as the dancers stood arrested far upstage, their backs to the audience, their arms outstretched to the light among the trees. Now there was only the low throb of drums, a pulse of darkness almost below the threshold of hearing. Then, threading its way through the drumbeats, a melody of aching sweetness came, and with it a girl draped in the thin veils of spring. She advanced to the center of the enormous platform and captured its spaces with the movements of her body. To Bren's mind came the thought of a spell — an intricate fabric of gesture and motion woven in the shimmering emptiness of the stage. If Erika said to herself, Perfection; every move is perfect, every tiny angle of wrist and toe, of neck and shoulder and knee, Bren thought, Magic. Enchantment.

The music changed again, and the young men turned, their ferocity transformed into longing and desire. They swept around the girl in ever-decreasing circles, but when it seemed

71

that at last they must seize her, she broke away with a movement as simple and strong as a gust of wind and left them in a knot of upraised arms, clutching thin air as the light faded around them.

Erika produced an audible sigh in the silence that followed the last low drumbeat. Then everyone was applauding. When it was possible to speak, she said, "You realize you just saw something very special?"

Bren nodded. Even without any standard of comparison, he knew that this was true.

"The rest will be a letdown," Erika said. "At least I think it has to be, but that gave me goose bumps."

"Are you cold?" Bren asked, giving the blanket a half-hearted poke.

"That's not what I meant, but yes. Now that you mention it. Hush. Here they go again."

As the lights dimmed for the next number, Bren shook out the blanket and tossed half of it over Erika, who pulled it up to her chin and moved closer to him. Any anxiety about his next move was forgotten as he watched the fascinating activities on the stage. The second ballet could not have been more different. A man in what must have been a very flexible business suit entered holding a telephone. Hope, frustration, despair, and finally success were clear in every move as he tried to reach his girlfriend, who now appeared on the opposite side of the stage dressed in a filmy nightgown and also holding a telephone. They danced the stormy progress of their conversation, and the audience laughed delightedly.

A group of spirited folk dances followed. Erika moved closer as the temperature dropped, and Bren put his arm around her. It now seemed the logical thing to do. Before the program was over, his free hand was holding hers, and they were sending each other signals of delight in the performance and in each other's company.

In the big kitchen on Eighty-fourth Street, Rose washed the dishes from a frugal meal, and Miranda gazed pensively into the dying fire. Shadow paced the floor and whined, his nails clicking on the tiles. Finally he came and laid his head in Miranda's lap, something he had never done before. "Well, Shadow," she said. "Are we lonely? Are we jealous, or what?" The dog thumped his tail. "Boys grow up, you know," Miranda continued. "They even grow away from their dogs. Oh, yes, they do. You'd better believe it."

"You're a disgrace," Rose said. "How you ever managed to send him to camp I'll never understand."

"That was different," Miranda said, "but don't worry. I'll be good."

"You'd better be," her mother said. "Now go to bed, and I mean to bed. Keep out of your studio or you'll be interfering before you know what you're doing."

"Never. I wouldn't dream of it. I'll go to bed with a silly book. Come, Shadow. We'll keep each other company." Miranda rose and swept out of the kitchen with the disconsolate dog trailing behind her.

In the shadowy courtyard of the Apthorp, Bren and Erika stood holding hands, as they had walking through the park and down Seventy-ninth Street. The curtains were drawn across the few lighted windows, and the doorman dozed in his chair by the gate. Erika shivered in the sharp air, and Bren pulled her close. It was at this moment that he heard his mother call, strongly and unmistakably in the one clear channel of his mind that was always open to her. He stiffened and drew back, and Erika, startled, did the same.

"Oh, damn!" he said. "Damn, damn, damn damn." At the same time he clutched his head, which was perhaps the best thing he could have done.

"What is it?" Erika begged. "You look terrible."

"Headache," Bren mumbled. "Really fierce. I get them sometimes. I'm sorry. It was such a perfect evening."

"Yes, it was. Totally perfect," Erika said, but the spell was broken now, and a good three feet separated them. "Are you going to be all right? What do you do for them?"

"I've got some pills at home," Bren lied. "It goes away very fast. Don't worry. Really. It's disappearing now." He took a step forward, but the mood was not to be recaptured.

"Go home," Erika said. "It might come back. You really had me worried, Bren. Call me tomorrow and tell me how you feel."

"Don't mother me!" Bren cried, suddenly furious with the whole world of women. "I've got one mother too many now."

"And that's a pointless remark, if I ever heard one," Erika said.

"Yes, it is. I know it is, and I'm sorry. What a disgusting end to a marvelous evening. I'd better go before I make it worse." He turned and blundered out of the courtyard.

"See you . . ." Erika said in a small, forlorn voice that trailed away into the now-dreary splashing of the fountains.

Chapter Nine

Bren stopped at the corner of Seventy-ninth and Broadway.
I won't go home, he thought. If I do, I'll kill her, and besides,
it would mean that I came when I was called. It was eleven
o'clock. The thought of a long walk either up or down the
familiar length of Broadway held small appeal, and it was too
late to visit Eli. I'll go see Dad, Bren said to himself. Maybe
I'll even stay. He's always asking me to, and that'll teach her
a lesson. He set off at a brisk pace toward Central Park.

Bren had never been in the park this late, never, in fact,
after dark except when a stream of concert- or play-goers
filled the now deserted walks. The way was as well lighted
as ever, but the heavy trees seemed to crowd closer to the path
and hang their shaggy heads over the lamps, casting deep
shadows between the pools of light. It's only about three
blocks wide, he told himself (three long crosstown blocks),
and plunging his hands into his pockets, he strode eastward
through the park.

The worst places were the dark underpasses. At the end of
the last one a huge figure loomed, black against the lamplight
on the path. Bren's heart thundered in his chest; he tried to
whistle, but found he had lost the knack. "Peace, brother,"

said a soft voice as he came out of the tunnel, and he saw a tall black man in a sweat suit waiting while an absurdly tiny, moplike dog snuffled in the dry leaves.

"Peace," Bren said, and hurried on.

The streets of the East Side were deserted at this hour — clean, empty, devoid of life. It was possible to think of something besides being jumped on from behind a tree. Inevitably Bren thought of Erika and was surprised at the sharp stab of pain that went through him at the image of her small, bewildered face. She had been hurt by his abrupt departure. He should have stayed, letting the force of his mother's call fade from his mind.

So I had a sudden headache, he said to himself, and it went away. So I could have said, Sorry! and gone back to hugging her. She wasn't mad; she was worried about me. The idea of himself as a heroic sufferer from some obscure malady — perhaps a brain tumor — was appealing. But I had to blow it, he concluded angrily, and wondered if he would be given another chance. The thought of Erika's fragile ribcage within the circle of his arm as they sat in the theater drove him to such despair that he walked half a block past his father's building.

In spite of having visited his father many times, Bren always had trouble finding the right buzzer for the apartment. There were at least a hundred of them, and they were in no discernible order. 4-F followed 7-C, which followed 16-G. As he searched, the doorman, privately christened "Smirky Sammy" by Bob West, came up behind him and watched his struggles.

"Your dad's got company," Sammy observed just as Bren finally located the buzzer.

Bren jumped and lost his place on the bell panel. "What kind of company?" he asked.

"The kind of company you don't want to be interrupted with," Sammy said, with one of the knowing grins that had earned him his name.

"It must be fun to know everybody's business," Bren said.

"That's what I'm paid for," said the doorman.

"I thought you were paid to keep out thieves and poor old bag ladies who might want to sleep in the lobby," Bren said, "but who cares? I was only passing by. If my father has company, I'll come another time."

Bren turned and stamped out onto Third Avenue. He was very angry and, he now realized, both cold and tired. The long, cheerless walk back to the West Side seemed impossible. But now it occurred to him that it was unnecessary, and he turned toward Seventy-ninth Street and the luxury of a crosstown bus.

It was nearly midnight by the time he got home. The house was dark and unusually silent. Everyone seemed to have gone to bed, even Shadow, who usually filled the front hall with his overwhelming welcome as soon as the key touched the lock. A dim light filtered down from the landing above, and with its aid Bren climbed the stairs. He was conscious of feeling both relieved and somewhat abused by this lack of reception. I could have stayed out all night, he thought, for all they care.

When he reached the landing, however, his mother's door opened, and there she stood in an old bathrobe, her face white and distraught, the dog trying to push her out of the way. "Where have you been?" she cried. "I've been worried out of my mind. The ballet must have been over for hours."

"I went for a walk," Bren said.

"For a walk. You went for a walk? How can you just stand there and say you went for a walk when I've been wondering whether to call the police?" Miranda ran her hands through her already disordered hair and turned back into the bedroom, where she began to pace the floor.

Bren had little choice but to follow her. He put a restraining hand on Shadow's head and stared at his mother. She certainly looked much less like a witch and much more like a mother than he was accustomed to. Was it an act? Clearly not, but he was still unwilling to forget the incident that had driven him to walk the streets.

"Mom, I am sixteen years old," he said. "Suppose I had decided to take my date somewhere after the ballet. So what? You never mentioned that there was a curfew. Next time let me know, and I'll take it into account. I might even telephone, although I doubt I would have tonight. Not under the circumstances. I'm sure you know what I mean."

"I haven't a clue," Miranda said distractedly. "I don't know what you're talking about. Why shouldn't you telephone? It was the least you could have done."

Bren studied her in silence. Was it possible she had really forgotten the summons? Not likely, he thought, but she was probably unaware of the effect it had had on the final moments of his evening with Erika.

"You promised not to summon me," he said finally, "but you couldn't resist, could you, and it really pissed me off."

Miranda looked stricken. "Oh, Bren," she said, "did I really? I didn't mean to. I must just have been thinking hard about you — hoping you were having a good time, you know, and all that sort of thing."

78

She had made a mistake, and Bren found himself angrier than ever. "Sure, Mom. If I'd believe that I'd believe anything. What do you take me for," he shouted, "some sort of mental defective? I know how much concentration you put into calling me, and you did it tonight at approximately ten minutes after eleven, and it made me so mad I almost didn't come home at all. I went to see Dad," he finished vindictively.

"So why didn't you stay?" Miranda cried. "Why didn't you stay and let your mother worry all night instead of just an hour or two?"

"Because he had company, that's why. He had the kind of company you don't want to be interrupted with, to quote his repellent doorman. Not really wanting to sleep in the park, I decided to come home." Bren was appalled to see the effect this explanation had on his mother, but it took him a minute to figure out what he had said that would account for it.

Miranda sank into a chair and covered her face with her hands. "I knew it," she said. "I knew there had to be someone else. Why else would he leave and not want to come back?"

Bren himself had not really confronted his father's apparent infidelity; he'd had too much else on his mind. Now he was struck dumb in a tangle of conflicting emotions. Worst of all, he was obviously expected to say something manly and comforting to his mother. Nothing whatsoever came to mind.

"So that's that," Miranda said in a small, husky voice, which was alarmingly on the verge of tears.

"So that's what?" Bren asked, playing for time.

"Oh, Bren, don't be stupid!" his mother cried, jumping up

with a startling return to her usual manner. She strode to the window and stared out toward the park and the East Side, where her estranged husband presumably was disporting himself with some showgirl or feeble-minded, long-legged secretary. "Not for long, he won't," she muttered. "Just give me time to think, and I'll fix that romance. I'll turn her into a toad."

"Come on, Mom," Bren said. "You can do better than that. A toad! You must have been reading fairy stories."

Miranda turned and stared at her son as if she had forgotten he was there. "Well, what do you suggest?" she asked.

"I suggest you forget the whole thing," Bren said. "I'm really sorry I said anything. You know what a cesspool Smirky Sammy has for a mind, or maybe you don't, but take my word for it. Dad's probably working late with someone from the office, whipping up a new campaign or whatever, and besides . . ." He had been about to add that Bob West was a man living alone, parted from his wife, and not a monk. Just in time, he thought better of it.

"Besides what?" Miranda asked suspiciously.

"Besides you shouldn't jump to conclusions," Bren improvised. It occurred to him that his mother's wrath had been redirected and that angry as he still was about her interference with his evening, a tactful withdrawal was now in order. He began to edge toward the door.

"I'll think of something," Miranda said. "I'll take my time and do it right. Maybe you can find out what she's like, Bren. That's such a help. I mean, if you want to make someone's hair fall out, for example, it helps to know what kind of hair it is. It's not essential, but it helps."

"Mom, if there is a person, you know, the kind of person

you're imagining, which I doubt, but if there is, I don't think I'm likely to meet her. Come on, Shadow, let's go to bed. I'm beat." I really am, he thought. What a day.

"You don't want to help," Miranda said, and the tears were back in her voice. "First you scare me half out of my mind, and then you refuse to do just a little tiny thing to help me. I can't believe it."

Bren, somewhat against his better judgment, crossed the room and gave his mother a hug. "I'm sorry I scared you," he said. "I didn't think of it that way, and as for the other thing, if I find anything out, I'll let you know, okay?"

Miranda returned the hug. She was comforted, if not convinced, and Bren and Shadow made their escape.

Chapter Ten

Bren slept badly and woke far earlier than was decent on a gray Sunday morning. A great chance to sleep, he told himself sternly, but it was no good. He was awake, and he was thinking about Erika and his mother and his father and his father's possible girlfriend. None of these subjects was in the least restful. With a growl that startled his still-slumbering dog, he threw back the covers and stumbled out of bed.

The kitchen was nearly dark except for the light over the stove, which revealed an array of dismantled burners and the rear end of Louise, who was either gassing herself or cleaning the oven. The thought of a peaceful and solitary cup of coffee would have to be abandoned. Bren snatched up Shadow's water bowl, slammed it down on the edge of the sink, and turned the cold water on full.

Louise emerged from the oven. "Hi, babe," she said. "You sure up at the dawn crack."

"So are you," Bren said crossly. "I was hoping for a cup of coffee, but I guess it's going to be that kind of day."

Louise sat down and regarded him amiably. "Won't be long now, babe. I been whacking away at this old monster since six o'clock, and she almost clean or as clean as she ever going to be. Gonna ask your daddy for a new stove one of these days, just see if I don't. One of those that cleans itself."

"Lots of luck, Louise," Bren said. He put the water bowl down and poured some dry dog food into another. "Here, Shadow. Be grateful your breakfast doesn't have to be cooked."

"Oh, your daddy's not so bad. His bark a whole lot worse than his bite."

Bren perched on the edge of the counter and studied Louise. Even though he had known her all his life, she continued to surprise him. "I thought you couldn't stand him," he said.

"As men go, he got a lot to recommend him," Louise said. "I just put him down to put our lady's back up, and maybe she see she can get along without him, too — like if she could get the idea he was no great bargain after all."

"I don't think it works that way," Bren said. "And I also doubt that foul-tasting mixtures of rhino horn work very well the other way."

"There's things you don't know. There's a pile of things, and you never will, even if you see it happen right under your nose. You not one of us, Bren babe, and I guess that good, but don't you doubt what you don't know nothing about." Louise took a halfhearted swipe at the oven door but continued to gaze at Bren with her small, dark eyes. "You look peaked," she finished. "What's the matter?"

"Nothing," Bren said, but there was something about Louise that made him want to confide in her almost against his will. "I'll tell you one thing, though, I know she can do," he went on reluctantly. "She can still call me when I'm someplace else, and it drives me up the wall."

Louise nodded. "Mind power. She best at that, and that not even proper witchery."

"I don't care what you call it, I don't like it. I feel like some kind of puppet, Louise."

"What you got to understand, Bren, is your momma is a *momma* first before she a witch or anything else." Louise laughed. "How many mommas you think would like to be able to call they babies the way Miranda call you? About a hundred percent, that's how many. Instead they got to nag and carry on. Maybe you lucky, ever think of that?"

"No," Bren said. "I didn't and I'm not about to. It's a howling nuisance and it's . . . embarrassing sometimes. I wish she'd just stick to her spells and potions."

"For spells you better come to me," Louise said. "Miranda careless when it come to spells. She cast a fine spell when she concentrate, but you can't just count on her to do all the little things in the right order. You want to charm a girl and be sure it work, you come to old Louise LaReine."

Bren jumped off the counter. "Stop that," he shouted. "I don't want to charm a girl, and furthermore I never will. Come on, Shadow. We'll have a walk to the deli and get me some breakfast. It's too early in the morning for all this garbage."

Louise chuckled and put her head back in the oven, but Bren's exit was foiled by the arrival of Madame Lavatky. Wrapped in an ancient peignoir trimmed with scraps of ermine and peacock feathers, she appeared in the doorway and cut off his escape.

"Stop, thief!" she cried, and pointed an accusing finger at him. He stopped, puzzled at this display of hostility from an admirer. His head was beginning to ache. "I come for my beautiful book which you take and do not return," continued the singer, seeming to tremble with indignation.

"She come to see what she can snatch from the kitchen before anybody else get up," Louise said.

"You lie, black fiend," cried Madame Lavatky. "Never have I been so insulted. What use have I for your decimated tea bags? I who drank tea with the Empress of all the Russias?"

"Tea, was it?" Louise said. "That a damn sight better than lamb chops."

"I'll get your book," Bren said, and fled up the stairs, nearly tripping over Luna, who was stretched completely across one of the top steps.

He came down cautiously with the heavy volume, skipping the tread where the cat still lay. Luna snarled quietly as he went by. "You were such a nice kitten," Bren said over his shoulder. "What went wrong?"

Madame had retreated from the kitchen and was waiting for him in the hall. "My dear young man," she said. "There was no need for such rushing. Did I not say keep it forever if you wish? Keep, study, enjoy the so beautiful arts of the Ballet Russe. We who know of the finer things," and she cast a malevolent glance toward the kitchen, "we must share. Is it not so?"

"Thank you, Madame Lavatky. I'm sure it is, but I've finished with your book. Maybe I'll borrow another one sometime, but now I absolutely have to go out and get some breakfast," Bren said, and snatching Shadow's leash from its hook by the door, he escaped from the house.

The day was even more dismal than it had seemed from inside, foggy and dank with a chill that made Bren shiver in his light jacket. He thought of going back when Shadow had had his walk. Maybe Louise would have finished the stove by then, and he could settle down with his breakfast and a book in the kitchen. But maybe she wouldn't have. It was just as likely that she and Madame Lavatky would go back to their exchange of insults and that the kitchen would be uninhabitable. Bren tugged Shadow toward Broadway. Having the dog with him made breakfast a problem. He knotted the leash around a small tree in front of the deli, bought coffee and a doughnut, and carried them out to eat on the sidewalk.

The Apthorp was directly across the street. Bren leaned against a lamp post, sipping his coffee and contemplating, through the tall iron gates, the scene of last night's disaster. He looked at his watch. Nine o'clock. Just the time on a Sunday morning when sensible people were stretching luxuriously between the sheets and turning over for another snooze. Brief though their friendship had been, Bren could easily imagine Erika in the sensuous enjoyment of her last few hours in bed. He thought of her face, with the covers pulled up to her nose, the dark lashes lying against high cheekbones, the incongruous bright hair tousled against the pillow. Then he thought of the rest of Erika, slim and wiry like a little cat, curled contentedly in an oversized bed. What was he going to do with himself until it was a civilized hour to make a phone call? Bren sighed, threw his coffee cup into a litter basket, and untied Shadow's leash.

"Let's go down to the river, old boy, and wallow in misery for a while," he said, and headed for Seventy-ninth Street and the two long blocks sloping down to the Hudson. They crossed Riverside Drive into the park and took the path that went under the highway. Shadow tugged at his leash, impatient for the waterfront with its pigeons and gulls and wonderful smells. They went down the curving steps leading to the great stone rotunda. Here there was a shallow fountain where in summer a circle of bronze turtles spouted thin streams of water. It was a favorite wading pool for dogs and children, but Shadow, recognizing its present uselessness, pressed on toward the river. Bren unsnapped the leash; there were no more streets to cross and probably no policemen to object to a dog's freedom on this unpromising Sunday morning.

Leaving Shadow to his adventures, he walked to the rail and stared gloomily at the multitude of small craft swaying slightly in some imperceptible current beneath the still, dark surface of the water. The masts of the sailboats were wrapped in fog, and the sleek sides of the speedboats glistened with moisture. Then Bren saw that one touch of color enlivened the scene. An old houseboat was anchored close to the shore, and in its peeling superstructure was a window from which warm yellow light shone through a frill of red curtains. What a way to live, he thought: just me and Shadow and some nice girl (Erika, of course) floating by ourselves on the river.

Bren turned reluctantly from this vision of cozy independence to check up on his dog and saw that he was no longer alone. A small figure, instantly recognizable in spite of being muffled in a huge black hooded sweatshirt, was leaning on the rail not ten feet away. He felt a suffocating surge of terror and joy and incredulity. Even a life spent with the everyday practice of magic had not prepared him for such serendipity.

"Erika!" he shouted. "I thought you'd be asleep."

She turned, a wide, silver grin flashing out of the black hood. "I wondered when you were going to see me," she said. "What a funny coincidence. I thought you'd be asleep, too. Everybody else seems to be. It's weird down here, and there's this huge black dog scouting around by himself."

"No, he's mine," Bren said, laughing. "That's Shadow. I forgot you hadn't met."

"Good name. He's like something mythological flitting between the trees."

"Yes, well, he's like a shadow, and he follows me like a shadow, but you'll find he's all too real, if he takes to you."

"Is he likely not to take to me?" Erika asked.

"If he doesn't, it will be a first," Bren said. "You shouldn't be flattered by Shadow's approval, but it's nice to have just the same." Bren whistled, and the Newfoundland came bounding out of the mist. He gave Erika only the briefest examination, and then he licked her chin, something he was able to do merely by stretching his neck with all four feet on the ground. Erika stood very still, looking both pleased and terrified.

"You're not used to dogs," Bren said, astonished that this should be true of someone he felt so close to.

"I've never had a pet, not even a turtle."

"That's awful. Doesn't your father like animals?"

"I guess not. I used to ask for a kitten when I was little, but I never got one, so I gave up. Since he's hardly ever home, I can't see what difference it would make."

"Is he home now?" Bren asked.

Erika shook her head. "He was out all night," she said. "He's got a girlfriend. He said we'd do something together

88

today, but who knows, and if it's going to be a threesome, forget it. I have half a mind to stay out all day."

"Let's stay out all day together," Bren said. "My father seems to have a girlfriend, too, and my mother is full of terrible plots for revenge."

Erika produced another of her dazzling smiles and pushed the hood away from her face. "Down with families," she said. "Here, Shadow, let's make friends. This is a threesome I can go for." She held out one hand, and the dog thrust his muzzle into her palm.

Bren pointed to the houseboat. "Just before I saw you, I was thinking how great it would be to live there by myself with Shadow and . . ." He hesitated. "Well, maybe one other very congenial person . . ."

For a long moment they stared at each other. Then Bren said, "My headache went away, incidentally, so let's turn the clock back, oh, about ten hours, I should think."

"To another headache?" Erika asked, moving closer to him.

"No," Bren said. "There won't be any more of those."

Her mouth was soft and her hardware barely noticeable, at least at first. Bren, whose experience so far had been confined to brief kisses at school parties or on the steps of brownstones after movie dates, discovered in the next few minutes many variations on the same fascinating theme. At last he simply held her close, his arms wrapped around her slim body, her face buried in his shoulder.

She lifted her head, looking a little dazed. "We have the whole day ahead of us," she said. "Just think of that."

"I am," he answered. "And it's clearing up."

Out in the harbor the clustered masts were emerging from the mist. On one a flag stirred and opened to the rising breeze, flaring into color with the first touch of sun. Behind them the wet branches of the trees shone silver in the new light growing in the east, and on the face of the river the fog rolled and broke, the gray water suddenly flashing blue.

They turned to walk along the waterfront, their arms entwined, the big dog ranging among the trees, the world brightening around them. Ahead stretched a day of infinite possibilities unfolding before them like a multicolored fan.

Chapter Eleven

October came, and Bren spent most of its brief golden days either in class or entombed in the theater. He made this sacrifice willingly, but not without regret. *Macbeth* and Erika claimed the time he would have spent squeezing the last good out of the park before winter's early dark changed everything.

Preparations for the play quickened toward its opening on November sixth, a date that now seemed terrifyingly near. Edward Behrens spent the hours after school in the cafeteria trying to persuade his young cast that the words of Shakespeare expressed the passionate lives of people as real as themselves. It was uphill work.

Meanwhile in the basement, the technical crew struggled with tasks at least as hard. How would the witches disappear into thin air or Banquo's ghost come and go in the crowded banquet hall? There were apparitions (four of them, all different) and a forest that got up and walked. These problems were added to others that were more conventional but hardly less daunting. A grim and solid castle was required.

Some scenes would take place inside, some out, and some both out and in. And all this had to be whisked away to give place to a barren heath.

The electrical wonders created by Eli and Bren were matched on the stage itself by the carpentry work of a blond giant named Jeremy, who had an uncanny way with canvas and chicken wire, and by Erika, who had somehow become chief carpenter's mate. Bren was not sure that he liked Jeremy, but he had little chance to find out. Dragging the heavy skeins of cable across the back of the balcony and listening to the hammering and laughter from backstage, he reflected bitterly on his original picture of himself and Erika working together day after day on the production of *Macbeth*.

But they still left school together and walked to Broadway through the autumn dusk. Sometimes they stopped off for coffee or ice cream before going home. On two successive Saturdays they worked in the theater, and on both Sundays it rained. There was no repetition of the idyllic day by the river, and Bren began to wonder if there ever would be.

Then one evening, as they stood indecisively on the corner, Erika said, "Hey, I know what, Bren. Come on home with me for a little bit. We can have a beer instead of all this legal slop, and you can see my place. Maybe you'll even get lucky and meet my old man."

Bren studied the last sentence for traces of irony, but was unable to decide whether Erika actually wanted him to meet her father or not. The proposal was curiously unappealing, especially since he was sure his beloved was one jump ahead of him and would soon be hinting at a reciprocal visit. Her interest in his home and family had not faded with time and evasion. Rather the contrary. Still, he was curious to know what lay beyond the Apthorp's courtyard and reluctant, as usual, to part from her after their short walk.

The front door of the apartment opened onto a huge circular foyer, with a mosaic floor laid out like one of his grandmother's charts of the zodiac. White walls with intricate moldings rose to a high ceiling. Living room and dining room opened off the foyer through arched doorways, the parquet floors gleaming softly in the dim glow from a single lamp. Erika went ahead, snapping switches, flooding the rooms with light. There was no sign of her father or, Bren thought, of anyone besides Erika in that luxurious space. Her boots and red umbrella, thrown down on some past rainy day, made a splash of color on the muted designs of the floor.

The kitchen was large and old-fashioned, but it lacked the warm, lived-in atmosphere of the room where Bren spent so much of his time. He wondered if anyone ever cooked or sat down to eat a meal with another person at the long glass table in the dining room. There was plenty of room but no place to eat in the kitchen.

Erika extracted two bottles of imported beer from the large and otherwise nearly empty refrigerator and opened them with a quick, irritable snap of the opener.

"Well, what do you think?" she said, with a vague gesture that seemed to include the rest of the apartment. "Neat, isn't it?"

"Fabulous," Bren said, "and huge." He thought that this notably smaller place seemed much bigger than the house he lived in. Obviously the occupants made a difference — the presence of so many overwhelming personalities, human and animal.

"Yeah, it's a lot of apartment for one and a half people," Erika said, "and you haven't even seen the bedrooms yet. Let's skip the bedrooms," she added. "They're just bedrooms except for mine, and it's just a mess. Come on, we'll sit in my favorite spot and drink these lovely things." She led Bren into the living room and over to the radiator window seat with its view of the Hudson. By an intricate and pleasantly intimate arrangement of their legs, they were both able to fit in the small space. Bren followed Erika's gaze and saw a new aspect of his river. The sky was not quite dark in the west. The lights on the Drive were a sparkling necklace along the shore. By craning his neck he could see the riding lights of the few boats that remained in the basin.

"I wonder if the houseboat's still there," he said. "It must be cold walking to it in the winter — wait till you feel the wind on Riverside Drive. But it's probably warm inside. They'll have a little space heater or maybe a pot-bellied stove."

"Better than this mausoleum, that's for sure," Erika said.

"I thought you liked it."

"I do. I like it a lot most of the time, and I like being alone, but enough is enough, you know?"

Bren nodded but found himself at a loss for words before this new, forlorn version of his girl. Their legs nestled warmly on the window seat, but she sat like a stone, her head turned away from him, her eyes fixed on the darkening horizon. Why had she brought him here? It seemed inconceivable to Bren that one's home could inspire such sadness. He wished suddenly that he could take her to West Eighty-fourth Street and install her in a niche by the hearth, there to be nuzzled by Shadow, snapped at by Rose, treated with queenly kindness by Miranda. After a moment, he did the only constructive thing he could think of. He reached over and took both of her hands firmly in his own. She looked at him now with an almost startled expression. "Erika," he said. "Cheer up. Come back from wherever you've been. It can't be so bad."

She started to get up. "I'm sorry. This should have been a good idea, but I guess it wasn't."

Bren slid to the floor and, turning, put his arms around her, but she wriggled free and walked out of the living room into the unfriendly, bright light of the foyer. "Dad could come home any time," she said. "Sometimes it would be nice to know when. Would you like another beer?"

"I haven't finished the first one," Bren said, gesturing toward the two bottles by the window.

"Do you want it?"

"No. I want to hug you and make you feel better."

"I wish it was that easy," Erika said.

It was clear to Bren that any notions he might have had of warm entanglements on the couch would have to be abandoned. He had been missing this sort of thing and wondered why she, apparently, had not. Still, the message was unmistakable. She was not only refusing physical consolation, she was refusing any consolation at all. He should take himself off, gracefully if possible. He gave her a small mock salute. "We strive to please," he said, "and seldom succeed."

"I'm sorry," Erika said again.

"Never mind," Bren said. "Maybe when this damn play is over, we'll get some time to just fool around or do something like the dance program. Who knows? If we live that long."

"Let's hope we won't have to wait till the play is over to have some fun," she said with a wan smile. She was drifting toward the door, and he followed her reluctantly. "What about Saturday? No, I've got to paint the battlements."

"And I have to start focusing," Bren said. "Sunday, then."

"We can live in hope." Erika opened the door into the hall, where, by a bit of bad luck, the elevator had just stopped.

"Going down?" the elevator man asked, and Bren was cheated of even the hope of a parting kiss.

"See you tomorrow in the slave market," he called as the door slid shut. Erika waved listlessly and turned back into her empty apartment.

She wandered into the living room again and stood staring at the two half-empty beer bottles standing deserted on the window seat. Depression was rapidly turning to rage, and she contemplated throwing one of them across the cold perfection of the room.

"What's the *matter* with me?" she said out loud. "I finally meet someone I really like, and I turn into some kind of shrinking violet." No boy she had ever known before would have put up with such behavior for two minutes, and surely even Bren's patience and understanding could not be limitless. "He'll think I'm hopelessly neurotic," she mumbled. "Not neurotic-interesting but neurotic-boring, and he'll be right." Instead of throwing the beer, Erika decided to drink it. She consumed both half bottles, staring moodily out the window, and felt her spirits faintly but perceptibly revive. He had not, after all, said anything that wasn't hopeful and encouraging. They would find something fun to do. They might even spend Sunday together. Erika put a favorite blues record on the stereo and lay down on the couch. It crossed her mind that if she had a dog like Shadow to come and lay his shaggy head on her chest, this solitude would be bearable. It was a short step to thinking about Bren's house, seemingly so full of people and animals. That's where we should have gone, she thought, even at the cost of a little privacy.

Erika was aware that Bren was not enthusiastic about taking her home. He had evaded her broadest hints, but boys were like that. They always tried to give the impression that they had been born, not of parents, but by some remarkable manufacturing process that presented them to the world fully formed, just as they were, without roots or antecedents. At least most boys did. This wasn't really fair to Bren, who talked quite a lot about his home, but always in a mysterious way, as if he had something to hide. Erika's curiosity began to revive, and with it came a trace of optimism. She got up and went to look out the window again, this time with eyes full of dreamy speculation. The music, sad but beautiful, crept into her bones, and she began to dance.

Chapter Twelve

Contrary to his gloomy predictions, Bren found that the next two days in the theater were more fun — more what he had imagined in the beginning. He was working on the stage, for one thing, hanging and focusing the long line of Fresnel lights that hung on a pipe just inside the front masking curtain. First he brought the pipe down onto the stage, where he could put the lights in roughly the right positions and connect the cables. It was positively luxurious to do this work with both feet on the floor. Even after the pipe was hauled back into place, he was able to stand on a short, sturdy ladder while Eli turned the lights on in pairs and called directions for focusing.

Erika worked almost at his feet, hammering nails with surprisingly deft strokes into an intricate network of wooden struts that would become a tower of the castle. Jeremy was in the shop constructing a banquet table with one false side, designed to conceal the actor who would play Banquo's ghost. When the changing of the lights made it too dark for Erika to see, she came to the foot of the ladder and talked to Bren. Her high spirits seemed to have returned completely.

They left the theater each night in a festive mood, but

this spirit of camaraderie was not, in the end, to Bren's advantage. On the evening of the second day, as they stood together on the corner, Erika made her bid for a return invitation. "It's too nice a night to just go home," she said. "Why don't we go over to your house for a change, and you can introduce me to Luna. Now that I've made friends with Shadow, a cat should be easy."

"That just shows how little you know about cats," Bren said, playing for time. If he had ever imagined a day when it might be even halfway safe to take her home, this particular one would have been low on his list.

His mother had risen early with a fanatical gleam in her eye and had gone to the phone to invite Bob to dinner. Bren could have told her that before breakfast was a bad time to ask his father anything, but surely she must know that. He fixed his own breakfast in the center of a cyclone, but was allowed to eat it in peace while Miranda went off, muttering darkly, to her studio. Then, as he warily climbed the stairs to fetch his books, he saw a purple haze drifting through the half-open door of the tower room and glimpsed his mother poring over an enormous tome under the fixed blue stare of Luna, who sat like a pharaoh's cat, paws together, encircled by her tail, on the edge of the desk. It was possible, but not likely, that conditions in the house on Eighty-fourth Street would have improved by nightfall.

Erika was looking stubborn, and Bren improvised hastily. "Tonight's no good," he said. "We just had the floors done. Mom said everything would be sticky, with just a tiny path from the front door to the bedrooms. I expect we'll have to go out to dinner. You couldn't see the house at all or sit down in the kitchen, which is really the neatest place."

"What about the animals?" Erika asked suspiciously.

"I don't know," Bren confessed. "Good question. They're probably shut up in the attic."

"I don't believe you," she said flatly. "I think you're making the whole thing up to keep me out of your house. Honestly, Bren, you'd think it was some kind of chamber of horrors with skeletons in the corners and bats flitting around."

Bren was indignant. "What an idea. Who would want to live with a lot of bat droppings all over the place?"

"Who indeed?" Erika said. "But until I see it, that's what I'm going to think."

"Well, you're just going to have to think the worst for a few days. I hear this floor stuff takes ages to dry."

"That's just about the stupidest thing I ever heard," Erika said. "But never mind. I get the picture, Bren, and don't worry. I won't ask again." She turned and started off down Broadway.

"Erika!" Bren cried. "Wait a minute. You don't understand."

"That's what you think," she called over her shoulder, and swung away down the crowded sidewalk.

Bren stood on the corner looking after her in despair. He wondered briefly if it wouldn't have been better to take her home, then shuddered at the possibilities. He would open the living room door to disclose his grandmother crouched over her crystal ball, or Louise would be sweeping the hall in the full splendor of her purple dashiki. Madame Lavatky would be climbing the scale to her shattering high C, and the door to the studio would be open upon a scene of some inexplicable weirdness. The situation was impossible and could only get worse. Bren cursed himself for the feebleness of his lie. It had seemed quite inspired as a spur-of-the-moment effort, but he would have to do better. If I ever get a chance, he thought as he turned toward home. If she ever believes a word I say or even wants to try.

The next day was Saturday, and Bren endured a full after-noon in the theater with Erika. She seemed, in paint-spat-tered black jeans and sweatshirt, more attractive than ever, an effervescent, elfin girl whose gaiety was dispensed in equal measure to all three of her fellow technicians. He had become no more special than Eli or Jeremy or probably even the janitor. He ground his teeth and struggled with the big floodlights in front of the backdrop. Eli was being unusually hard to please. Bren thought the ghastly afternoon would never end, and when it did, he returned from the lighting storage room to find that Erika had gone.

Sunday's weather was heartbreakingly fair. "I am not go-ing to call her," Bren said to Shadow as they wandered from tree to garbage can in the shimmering early morning light. "She'll have to call me, and she'll have to be quick about it. We're not going to waste this day, old friend, waiting for some girl to call." Shadow wagged his tail and looked hope-fully toward the park. Five minutes later Bren was back in the kitchen at the phone, listening to Erika's phone ring and ring and ring. It was hard to imagine that neither Erika nor her father was home at this hour on a Sunday, but after about twenty rings, he had to conclude that they were either out or had turned off the bell.

Bren sat down to a gloomy and solitary breakfast. Before he had finished, the telephone rang and sent him dashing across the kitchen with a pounding heart, but it was only his father.

"What's the matter?" Bob asked. "You sound like you've lost your best friend. How about brunch?"

"Brunch?" Bren growled. "I just finished breakfast."

"Not now, for God's sake. I'm still in bed. I was thinking of something civilized like one o'clock."

"That's lunch," Bren said, "but never mind. I know, I know. You don't have to tell me about brunch in New York. Isn't it too nice a day to spend inside some restaurant?"

"Come on, Bren. I know a new Mexican place — tacos, chili, margaritas. You'll love it, and I want you to meet a friend of mine."

So that's it, Bren thought. Terrific. Tacos and margaritas (which he probably wouldn't be allowed to have) and his father's new girlfriend. His mind raced, trying to come up with a good excuse, but in the end he couldn't refuse his father. "Okay," he said into the phone. "Thanks, Dad. Just tell me where and when."

Bren went back to his breakfast, now cold, and finished it with a kind of grim determination. He was not hungry but felt an obscure need to fortify himself for whatever the unpromising day might bring. As the last crumb of toast went down, his mother came in. She was wearing her old bathrobe, looking frazzled and friendly. Calling a cheerful good morning, she went to the refrigerator and, to Bren's consternation, produced a quart of pancake batter and a package of bacon.

"I was looking for you upstairs," she said. "How nice you're still here. We can have a real old-fashioned Sunday morning breakfast. You didn't eat much, did you?"

"Eggs, toast, and juice," Bren said. "I'm sorry, Mom."

"You can eat a few pancakes, I'm sure. Boys your age are bottomless pits." Miranda began putting an alarming quantity of bacon in a large frying pan. She seemed happy as a lark. Bren loosened his belt and resigned himself to being a good son. Sometimes he felt that pleasing his parents was a full-time job, all the more so since they had taken to leading separate lives.

Breakfast, nevertheless, was a pleasant meal, except for the growing discomfort of his stomach. Miranda was interested in the play and managed to talk about it without once alluding to its witchy aspects. Bren found he had more to say about stage lighting than he would have thought possible. It was almost the first time he had thought about lighting as an activity divorced from its associations with Erika. He expounded, and his mother, who could be a good listener when she chose, took in every word. It was only as he was struggling out of his chair, intent on reaching the park in time to walk off his second breakfast, that he made a false move.

"That was great," he said. "Just don't plan too much for supper. I'm already two meals ahead, and in a couple of hours I have to have brunch with Dad."

Miranda stopped on her way to the sink. "Brunch?" she said. "Lucky you. I didn't think your father was into brunches."

"I didn't either," Bren said cautiously, "but I guess he is. I whined about going to the park on such a nice day, but he was determined, and I decided to humor him."

Miranda sighed. "Well, I wouldn't mind going in your place. I never go anywhere these days, but I suppose he wouldn't appreciate the substitution."

"Not perhaps this time," Bren said unwisely.

"What's special about this time?" Miranda snapped.

"Nothing, so far as I know. Don't jump to conclusions."

"Who's jumping to conclusions?" she cried. "I suppose he's bringing his paramour."

"What a silly idea," Bren said. "And what a silly word. Nobody has paramours anymore."

"That's what you think," Miranda said. "And just remember, Bren. If she's there, you know what I want." She brightened suddenly. "Maybe you could actually get a strand of hair. You could snag it on the sleeve of your jacket."

"I'm wearing a T-shirt," Bren said, "and besides, no one else is going to be there, Mom. You're making this whole thing up."

"We'll see about that," Miranda said darkly.

In spite of the brilliant October sunshine, the Mexican restaurant was dim, its windows shrouded by heavy orange curtains printed in black with scowling images of Aztec deities. The walls and ceiling were more cheerfully adorned with a vast collection of Mexican artifacts — clay jugs, baskets, masks, candlesticks, tin mirrors, and colorful weavings.

Bren took all of this in before he found his father in the farthest corner of the room. Bob West was not looking for his son; he was leaning across the table, which was surely too small for three, and gazing into the eyes of a woman with red hair. I could turn around and leave, Bren thought, and they'd be halfway through dessert before they realized I hadn't come. Curiosity, however, held him, and while he stared, a hostess in Mexican costume asked him if he was meeting someone.

"My father," Bren said, "over there in the corner," and allowed himself to be led to the third place at the tiny table.

Bob jumped, nearly knocking over the tall, frosty glass in front of him. "Bren, oh good. You're here. This is Alia. Alia, this is Bren."

A dazzling smile illuminated the thin, dark face of Bob's companion, and she reached both hands out to Bren, who had all he could do to refrain from shrinking back in his chair. "*Ma che bello!*" she cried. "Bobby, you did not tell me. He is the image of you. So like! How happy I am to see him at last."

At last? Bren thought. How long has this been going on? "Hi, Alia," he said, and gave her outstretched hands a perfunctory squeeze. He was startled to see that his father's face had turned bright red.

Bob took a hasty swallow from his drink. "We started ahead of you, old boy. I hope you don't mind. Not that you're late. We were a bit early. Waitress, another margarita, please."

The waitress, who had been hovering nearby, stared at Bren with beady black eyes, shrugged, and turned toward the bar.

His father's mistress (there no longer seemed any point in hoping that she was anything else) continued to gaze rapturously at Bren. Her eyes were very dark and, along with her olive skin and sharp, Mediterranean features, contrasted strangely with her furiously red hair.

"Alia's from Italy," Bob contributed proudly, as if he had

been unusually clever in acquiring an Italian girlfriend.

"From the Veneto," Alia said, "where there are so many people with red hair like mine. Perhaps you did not know this?"

"Lucky you," Bren said. "I've always wanted to go to Venice."

Alia sighed dramatically. "Ah, it is beautiful. You cannot imagine, but in New York I find so much more." She turned her smile once more upon Bob and then switched it back to Bren, who was unpleasantly reminded of a searchlight. His drink arrived, and Alia raised her glass. "To my new friend, Ben," she said, "and to my so good old friend, Bob. Such wonderful American names!"

Bren raised his glass. "It's Bren," he said, "with an *r*, but thanks anyway. *Salute*."

Alia clapped her hands. "Adorable! Don't tell me, Bob, he speaks Italian. I will love him instead of you, if he speaks Italian."

"That would be news to me," Bob said. "Do you speak Italian, Bren?"

"Of course not. Everybody knows a few toasts." Bren took a swallow of his margarita, a drink that was new to him, and found its curious mixture of salt and lime appealing. He wondered if there was much alcohol in it and decided to drink some more quickly and find out.

Alia turned the full force of her personality back to his father, and now, as she reached a slender hand to pluck at his sleeve, Bren saw her enormous ring. It was silver, intricately engraved with some kind of script that was at once strange and familiar, and its unusually high crown was set with a dark red stone. He looked more closely and saw that

106

on one side was a little knob that looked like the clasp to a tiny box. Catching his gaze, she withdrew her hand quickly and put it in her lap, all the while laughing and chattering to Bob.

Intrigued, Bren turned his attention to the rest of her jewelry, meanwhile draining his drink. There was no doubt now about its alcoholic content, and he felt greatly fortified to face the rest of the brunch. Jewelry, he observed, must be one of Alia's weaknesses, and though he knew little about the subject, he was struck by the oddity of her ornaments. Both wrists were entwined with copper bracelets of serpentine design, and around her neck was a formidable necklace of rough-cut amber beads. Something was nagging at the back of his mind, something his mother had said one night when, dressing to go out, she had adorned herself with a different but equally ill-assorted collection.

Bren caught the eye of the waitress and pointed to his empty glass. She expressed the same silent disapproval and produced another margarita. This was a comfort but didn't seem to advance matters very much. "Hey, Dad," he said finally, when Alia paused for breath, "are we going to eat or just sit here getting soused all day?"

Alia produced a silvery laugh. "Always they are hungry, the *ragazzini*. Come, Bob, we must feed him before he disappears. What a shame that would be."

Bob seemed startled out of a trance. "Oh, hell, excuse me, both of you. Of course we're going to eat. What do you know about Mexican food, Bren?"

"I've had it before," Bren said, "quite a few times, in fact, with you and Mom."

"That's right. How could I forget? Try the guacamole.

That's avocado mashed with tomato and garlic and chili powder. And tacos. Those are tortillas rolled around chicken or beef, or other things, I guess, and fried. Tortillas are . . ."

"Dad, I know what tacos and guacamole and tortillas are," Bren said. "I've had them before. Remember?"

Bob clutched his head. "Of course you have. Where did we used to go? That little dump on Columbus. What was it called?"

"Emilia's," Bren said.

"Right. Emilia's. Ever been there, Ally? It's just a simple place, but fun."

"You take me there sometime, Bobby," Alia said, "and Bren will come too. But now I think we try the restaurant we are in before he dies of hunger."

"Well, come on then," Bob cried, heaving himself up from the table. "It's a buffet. Have anything you want, both of you."

This was good news to Bren. They trooped over to the buffet table, and he was able to make a reasonably small selection from its overwhelming display. He feared he would now hear a sprightly discourse on the failure of his appetite, but this must be borne, along with a lot of other annoyance, no doubt, before he could make his escape. The second margarita was having a less agreeable effect than the first. He felt slightly dizzy and indisposed toward even the small amount of food he had chosen.

His pickiness, however, went unnoticed. Alia proved to be a lusty eater and one who flirted as she ate, as if stuffing her mouth were an irresistibly seductive act. Bren found that his dislike of the woman had turned to loathing. He covered the remains of his refried beans with a large lettuce leaf and gazed fixedly past Alia. As he did so, his glance fell on the huge purse hanging from the back of her chair. It was partially open and very full. On one side he could see the bristle end of a hairbrush and in the brush a tangle of red hairs; some of them appeared to be quite loose and near the open mouth of the bag. Bren caught his breath. What Mom couldn't do with some of those, he said to himself. The numbing effect of the margaritas fell away, replaced by a feeling of heroic resolution. He pushed back his chair. "Where's the men's room, Dad?" he asked, moving into position next to Alia's bag.

This simple question seemed to strike her as wonderfully precocious. "Adorable!" she cried again and encircled his waist with her arm. Bren found his hand virtually thrust onto the hairbrush and was able to get away with quite a handful as he freed himself from the embrace of his mother's rival.

In the men's room he pocketed his prize and returned to the table in such excellent spirits that he was able to endure the remainder of the meal and even consume some food. Guessing that the other two might linger on far into the afternoon, he pleaded an overload of homework and rose to go. Bob wrenched his eyes from Alia with a guilty start. "Homework on a day like this?" he said. "I hope we haven't kept you from the park."

"That's okay," Bren said. "Maybe I'll do it in the park. Shadow will be bored, but you can't have everything. Thanks for the great meal, Dad. See you around, Alia."

"*Ciao, bellino.*" The long hands reached for him again, but he was halfway to the door.

Chapter Thirteen

Alone in the big house, Miranda wandered restlessly from room to room. Her mother seemed to have gone out. Shadow, curled in a corner near the hearth, slept the patient sleep of a dog whose expectations have been disappointed. Only the presence of Luna, who trailed behind her, and the spectral voice of Madame Lavatky gave evidence of life in the still center of the day.

Though sunlight slanted through the windows of every room, Miranda felt the afternoon to be darkening around her. She was uneasy and she felt unwell. Her night had been troubled by vaguely menacing dreams, but she had thrown them off in the interest of motherhood and pancakes. Now the object of these good impulses was gone, and the feeling of fear evoked by her dreams came back in force. "Someone is trying to do me harm," she muttered to the cat, and Luna growled deep in her throat. Miranda put her hand to her head. A sharp pain had just shot through it from temple to temple. Now it was gone, but it left a dull ache behind. Her stomach also hurt, as if something inside was trying to gnaw its way out. "Mustn't be paranoid," Miranda said in a loud, bright voice. "The bacon was probably over the hill, or the pancake batter. They tasted all right, but you can't be too careful." This, she knew, was whistling in the dark. You couldn't miss the taste of bad bacon, and she had never heard of anyone being poisoned by a pancake.

The house, Miranda had always thought, was well protected. There was a pentacle painted on the doorstep under the mat and a witch bottle of bent pins and nails buried under the rhododendron. Inside, over the door hung a horseshoe pointing up and a pair of antelope horns. Three iron nails, which Miranda had obtained from a coffin maker, if not from an actual coffin, were embedded in the door. Such measures were guaranteed to keep the inhabitants of the house safe from all ordinary manifestations of evil.

This, then, was something out of the ordinary, and Miranda felt her pains increase and her panic rise. The fact that she had no idea who could be after her did nothing to calm her nerves. A known enemy was vulnerable to counterattack by well-known methods. But this miasma of ill will was something else. Pausing on the second-floor landing, Miranda heard the front door open stealthily and then the sound of a rattling chain. The hair rose on the back of her neck, and her heart pounded. Then she heard the brief, joyous gallop of Shadow's feet, and the door closed again. Bren had come for his dog and left again without a word — without a report on his father and on the other person Miranda felt sure had been present at the brunch. And Bren would have been a comfort, though he was useless when it came to defense against the supernatural. I'll get Louise, she thought, turning back down the stairs. She'll know what to do.

Standing in near darkness outside the basement apartment, Miranda hesitated, feeling a strange reluctance to visit her old friend and colleague. At last she raised her hand and knocked lightly on the door. A brief silence was followed by the voice of Louise, shrill and strong. "Thing of evil, begone!" it cried.

Miranda sighed and opened the door. By the flickering light of four tall candles she saw the triple circle drawn in white on the black floor. Inside the circle was a pentagram, and inside the pentagram was Louise, sitting up very straight on the edge of a small camp bed and staring at her with sharp, fierce eyes. Miranda advanced to the edge of the outer circle, and Louise relaxed. "Whew, Miranda, babe, you sure give me a scare," she said.

"I'm sorry, Lou, I didn't know." Miranda gazed anxiously at her friend. Only a very frightened witch will go to the trouble to set up a circle of protection. It was a lengthy ritual that involved many purifications by fire and water and the repetition of innumerable spells summoning the spirits of earth, air, fire, and water to stand at the four corners where the candles burned and protect the one within the circle during the long, dangerous hours of the night. It was clear that Louise had prepared for a substantial siege. She had gathered together all her articles of magical practice — her wand, her ritual knife, and the thurible, from which rose a thin column of acrid smoke. In addition, there were many homelier items such as pillows and blankets, a bag of potato chips, an ice bucket from which protruded the tops of several beer bottles, a pile of magazines, and the telephone on a long cord.

"This is terrible," Miranda said. "I was going to ask you to help me set up a circle of protection, and now I find that you're inside one. Can we both be under attack? We don't have the same enemies, at least I don't think we do."

"You been bothering a old black crone up on a Hundred Fifty-ninth Street?" Louise asked. Miranda shook her head. "Got to be coincidence, then."

"I don't believe in coincidence," Miranda said, "but I don't know where mine's coming from. Oh, damn, Louise, I was hoping you would help."

"Well, I can't come out," Louise said. "You know that. But just 'cause I'm in here don't prevent me giving advice. What's scaring you, babe?"

"Pains all over and terrible dreams. A feeling that something's following me around the house." Describing her symptoms had the effect of exaggerating them, and Miranda shivered.

Louise leaned forward on the bed and studied her intently. "You done no harm to any other witch?"

"Not lately or knowingly," Miranda said.

"Maybe somebody you don't think could be a witch, be a witch just the same," Louise suggested.

"I don't think I've done anything to anybody in the last few weeks," Miranda said. "I've been trying to be good. Of course I've had frightful thoughts about Bob's girlfriend, but I don't even know what she looks like."

"That be it, then," Louise said with a satisfied smirk. "He probably still got a picture of you. You better find out more about that young lady damn quick."

"Oh, Louise, Bob would never go out with another witch. That would be the last thing he'd do. What would be the point?"

"Mark my word," Louise said and delved into the potato

113

chips. "Want a beer? I could chuck you one. Do you good."

"No thanks, Louise. I've got to work on my own circle. There's so much to do. Maybe Rose will come home and help. Why does she have to be away when I need her most? A fine mother she turned out to be." Miranda turned toward the door. "I hope you'll be all right. I'll check up on you in the morning."

Louise pulled a beer out of the ice bucket. "I be fine," she said, and then a look of consternation crossed her face. "Except for just one thing. Lucky you come along or I might have had to step out and undo it all."

"What's missing?" Miranda asked, alarmed. "What did you forget, Lou?"

"Opener," Louise said, staring at the dripping bottle in her hand. "Top drawer by the stove."

Miranda walked carefully around the outside of the circle and pawed through the jumbled contents of the drawer, finally producing the kind of simple opener known as a church key. She tossed it to Louise, who caught it and chuckled. "Church key," she said. "That a double good joke in here. Thanks, babe. You better go now. Got a lot to do before dark."

"I'm going. Wish me luck." Miranda retraced her steps and shut the door firmly behind her as Louise leaned back against her pillows with every appearance of contentment. "I wonder she can drink all that beer," she muttered as she climbed the stairs. "Probably has a chamber pot under the bed."

After several hours in the park with Shadow, Bren felt almost happy as he walked back to his house. He was an optimistic person, and his spirits were easily restored by sunlight and the quiet, undemanding presence of trees. It had occurred to him that asking Erika for another real date, something that would appeal to her and be totally disconnected from his house and family, might allow them to start over and return to the happiness of the day by the river. These hopeful speculations helped him forget his father's inexplicable attraction to Alia. Where would Erika like to go? What uniquely New York event could he offer her that would prove his devotion in spite of his steadfast refusal to take her home? It was late October, and at the end of the month came one of the city's most exciting events. "The Halloween parade," Bren said aloud. "She won't have seen anything like that in Philadelphia."

Cheered by this idea, he opened the front door and came upon his mother standing at the foot of the stairs, white-faced, wild-eyed like a cornered animal. "Bren!" she cried. "Do you have to sneak in and out like a thief? You scared me out of my wits."

Bren, who had entered with all his usual brio, was at once alarmed and indignant. "I can make more noise if you really want me to," he said, "but sometimes it's hard to do anything right. What's the matter? You look like you've seen a ghost."

Miranda clutched her head. "Please, Bren. You don't know what I've seen. You never did have any imagination. Seen a ghost, indeed. My God. If you only knew."

Bren had not lived with his mother for sixteen years without seeing her in this state several times. He sighed. "You're being haunted," he said. "That means you're going to shut yourself up inside a circle and not fix dinner."

"I have to get ready before dark," Miranda said. "You know that."

Bren glanced at the daylight still pouring through the skylight at the top of the stairs. "There's plenty of time," he said. "Come and have some tea and maybe the feeling will go away. I've had a hard day, too."

A trace of color returned to his mother's face as she remembered where he had been. Curiosity warred with fear, and curiosity won.

"Well, maybe just a quick cup," she said. "With lots of sugar. I'm sure I need it, but you'll have to fix your own supper or wait for your grandmother."

"I can cope," Bren said, "if worst comes to worst. Come on." He led the way into the kitchen and put the kettle on. Miranda sank into a chair and waited for the confidences she associated with the drinking of tea.

"Now tell me all about it," she said, the minute she had a steaming cup in her hand.

Bren smiled lazily. "Tell you all about what, Mom?"

"Bren, don't tease," Miranda cried. "You know what I mean."

"Well, let's see. Shadow and I went over to the Bethesda Fountain. There was a hippie there playing sixties stuff on the guitar. It was sort of neat but sort of boring. Shadow thought so too, so then . . ."

"Stop that this minute!" Miranda said, and Bren stopped.

"Oh, I know. You want to hear about brunch with Dad. Well, okay. That was really boring too — more boring than the park, but the place was nice. They had all this cheerful Mexican stuff hanging all over the place, and I got to have margaritas. Nobody seemed to mind, and they were amazingly good."

116

"What was she like, Bren?" Miranda said in a taut, ominous voice.

"Really skinny," he said, relenting. "And sort of odd-looking. I mean she had this dark skin and red hair and very peculiar jewelry. Her name is Alia, and she comes from Venice, or so she says. I really didn't like her, if that's any consolation. She was creepy and gushy at the same time."

"Tell me about this peculiar jewelry," Miranda said. "It must have been very peculiar indeed for you to notice it."

"Well, there was a lot of it," Bren said, "and it didn't seem to go together. She had a big necklace of lumpy yellow beads and copper snakes on her arms and this humongous silver ring that looked like it had a secret compartment in it." He stopped, noticing that his mother was smiling, a slow, contented, feline smile. "You like this part about the jewelry?"

"I like it very much," Miranda said. "It's hard to believe, but it explains everything." Suddenly she laughed out loud. "Your poor father, Bren. Haven't you realized? He's taken up with another witch, and I bet he doesn't even know it yet. She has a nerve wearing witch jewels to brunch. What an amateur. And red hair with olive skin? It's almost certainly dyed. Some people think you have to have red hair to be a witch, but of course it has to be natural, and even then it's no big deal. Oh, how I wish I could get my hands on even one little hair!"

Bren stood up and dug in the depths of his jeans, then held aloft the clump of tangled red hair. Miranda gave a cry of triumph and snatched it out of his hand. "You're wonderful, Bren. My God, what did you do? Scalp the poor woman?"

"It was in her hairbrush," Bren said. "It was sticking out

of this big purse she had hanging over the back of her chair. Really, Mom. It was like taking candy from a baby."

"I've underestimated you," his mother said admiringly. She got up and prowled around the kitchen. "This changes everything," she muttered. "I can switch to attack, and that's much more satisfying than moping away the night in a dreary old circle of protection. Let's see. I think I've got everything I need — black candles, wax, henbane . . ."

"What about dinner, Mom?" Bren said.

"Dinner? Who's hungry?"

"I'm hungry, and I think I deserve it," Bren said. "You don't do these things till midnight, anyway. Better eat something yourself and build up your strength."

"Spiritual strength is what I need," Miranda said. "I should fast, but never mind. Let's see what's in the fridge."

When Bren climbed the stairs that night, full of an assortment of leftovers and tired from an exceptionally trying day, he could hear his mother chanting in her tower room. He paused and peered through the tiny window in the door. Robed in black, tall and magnificent, her bright hair an incongruous halo in the flickering light of the black candles, she stood over the smoking thurible molding a small waxen doll — a doll with an untidy mass of dyed red hair. "Poor Alia!" Bren said, and went down the hall to his room.

Chapter Fourteen

A technical marvel, that's what it'll be, thought Edward Behrens. A technical marvel and an artistic catastrophe. Slumped in a seat near the back of the house, he was watching the technical crew transform a bare stage into a blasted heath in medieval Scotland. Although the basic lighting and sets were finished, much remained to be done in the way of special effects. He had just come from a disheartening rehearsal of his principal actors, who, it seemed, were simply too young to convey or even to understand the primitive evil that informed the black history of Macbeth. But the witches were already good. Why? he wondered, watching the innocent capers of Erika, who, momentarily out of a job, was turning cartwheels in front of the cauldron. Erika and, to a slightly lesser degree, her two co-witches hadn't far to go before they were truly terrifying.

These speculations were interrupted by the voice of Eli, who had opened the sliding window in the front of the light booth and was craning to see something in a far corner of the balcony. "We can't do much more until you've focused that light," he shouted. "What's the problem?"

"Problem?" said a strangled voice out of the shadows. "Why would there be a problem? Focused? I haven't even got the bastard hung yet. Is this play worth my life?"

"You'd better believe it," Eli said, and withdrew his head.

Erika stopped turning cartwheels and gazed in the direction of Bren's voice. She could just barely make out a dim figure suspended in space at the edge of the balcony, a gigantic, torpedo-shaped stage light swinging from its hand.

Technology, which had made such great strides with the electronic switchboard, had seemingly stopped when it came to getting the lights where they needed to be. Hanging and focusing remained in the early years of the industrial revolution.

Bren had one foot on the balcony rail and one hand on the steel pole that stretched upward from it and already held a cluster of lights and a tangled mass of cables and plugs. There was one space just above his head, and into that space, with a supreme effort, he managed to heave the forty-pound stage light. He got both feet on the balcony rail and propped the light on his shoulder while he attacked the C-clamp with his Crescent wrench. The clamp was frozen. Bren swore.

"What's the matter?" Erika called from the stage. "Are you all right?"

"I'm fine. Never better. What the . . . There, you unspeakable object. Take that." A ferocious blow freed the clamp, and Bren was able to attach the big light to the pole and point it roughly in the direction of the stage. He wrapped one arm around the support and searched the dark tangle of cables for an open plug. However, when light and plug were connected, nothing happened. "Eli!" he shouted. "Have I got power up here? I thought you were in a hurry."

Eli applied himself to his switchboard, and all over the house the spotlights began to pop on and off, flaring and fading in the gloom until finally Bren's light blazed under his hands. It would be too hot to handle in seconds, and he fished in his back pocket for gloves. "Lean over the cauldron from stage right," he called to Erika. "Kill everything else, Eli; I can't tell what I'm doing." In spite of its hazards and frustrations, Bren loved focusing. Three bolts, only one of them frozen, determined the position of the light. Four shutters, all sticky, narrowed it down to a hot spot on Erika's head. This was to be a special-effects spot that would turn the three witches red as they leaned over the cauldron. Once satisfied with the focus, Bren slid a red gel over the front of the light and was delighted with the effect it had on Erika's hair.

"That's good," Eli called. "You can come down now."

"You're a prince, Eli," Bren said, as he slid gratefully off the balcony rail and went down the stairs into the theater. It was good to feel solid ground under his feet.

"Was that dangerous?" Behrens asked. It had occurred to him that he had something more than an artistic responsibility for his young technicians.

"Only for you," Bren said cheerfully. "It's a good thing you didn't look up. You'd have had a heart attack. Erika, you should see what that light does to your hair."

"I can imagine," she said, joining him at the edge of the stage, "but I'm thinking of dying it green for the show."

"That's a disgusting idea. Have you thought that the show is only three nights, but your hair will be green for months?"

"I can dye it something else, if green palls."

"You'll be bald if you keep that up."

Erika ran one hand through the soft pink brush that adorned her head and looked thoughtful. "I hadn't thought of that," she said. "We could all three shave our heads and make up our faces like skulls. The only hair would be those awful, scraggly little beards. It would be a new interpretation."

"It would be gross," Bren said.

"It's supposed to be, and anyway, who asked you?"

The voice of Mr. Behrens rescued Bren from what seemed to be a doomed conversation. He came up front and shouted at the light booth, "Eli, let me see what you've got for this scene. Bren and Jeremy can be the other witches. Give me the lights and then let's try one of the projections. I stay awake nights wondering if this stuff is going to work. Jeremy!"

Bren clambered onto the stage, and Jeremy appeared yawning from the wings, where he had been napping on a pile of dusty curtains. His blond hair was becomingly tousled, and as he stretched, the muscles rippled under his skin-tight T-shirt.

"Crouch," Eli shouted. "You guys are a foot taller than the witches."

Erika held out her hand to Jeremy. "Make yourself small and ugly, if possible," she said, "and gather round the cauldron."

Bren supposed, miserably, that he should do the same. Behrens joined them and stood off to one side. "I'll be Macbeth," he said. "Go, Eli."

The stage darkened, and eerie blue and green lights came up around the cauldron, followed by Bren's red special.

"You'll have to give me more," Behrens said. "Even at the cost of a little atmosphere." The light brightened slightly on his face. "Now the bloody child, if you've got him. He's my

122

favorite, I have to admit." On the scrim behind the witches appeared the wavering apparition of a small, naked child streaked with blood.

"Macbeth, Macbeth, Macbeth. Be bloody, bold and resolute," Erika intoned in a suitably disembodied voice.

"Oh, lovely," said Behrens. "Thank you all *very* much. We're ahead in this department, which is just as well when you ponder the technical horrors of the play. It's not something you want to throw together at the last minute. I don't suppose you have something equally stunning for the first witch scene?"

"Wait till you see," Erika said. "Come on, Jeremy. Let's get that wicked tree."

"Cauldron off, tree on. Help me drag this thing, Bren." Jeremy heaved at one side of the cauldron, which seemed to be almost as heavy as it looked. "I'll have to put wheels on it or there's no way it's going to vanish into thin air."

"Please don't mention vanishing," the director said. "It's an issue I am simply not prepared to face."

"Don't worry. We'll think of something," Erika said.

The tree was new to Bren as well. Jeremy and Erika, he reflected bitterly, must have built it while he was hanging lights and disentangling cables in the remote corners of the balcony. It was a twisted skeleton, bare and desolate, its branches reaching out like claws.

"Now that is an evil tree," said Behrens. "That is an absolute nightmare of a tree. I love it. But the lights are different, I hope, or is that hoping too much?"

Eli's head appeared at the light booth window. "Would you wonderful people be changing scenes?" he asked. "I've still got work to do on the other one."

"Just a sketch, Eli — the barest suggestion of what you had in mind for this marvelous tree, and then I promise to go home and leave you all alone to your wizardry," said Behrens.

"It's not programmed yet," Eli said. "You'll have to wait while I bring them up manually."

The lights began to change around the four people on the stage. The red light went out, and the atmosphere grew cold and bleak. The backdrop now suggested a lowering, late afternoon sky. There would be rain, one felt, or something worse.

Behrens abandoned his pose as Macbeth and went out into the house. After a moment Bren joined him. It was hard to see the effect of the lighting from the stage, and the witch scenes were his own project. Eli had let him plot them and was going to let him run the cues once they were programmed into the board. He studied the stage, noting where the level of light was too high or too low and where in one place, instead of blending imperceptibly into one another, you could see the overlapping circles of two spotlights. It was still very good.

"Are you responsible for this miracle?" asked the director, and Bren nodded happily. "Well, only a few more humps to get over," Behrens went on. "Any ideas about these awful vanishings? We have to face it sometime in the next few days. We can do the old dry-ice trick, of course, but how to suddenly get a big enough puff of smoke to cover the witches' exit beats me. I don't think the budget runs to a real smoke machine in the wings. In fact, I'm sure it doesn't. We're way over as it is." (He refrained from mentioning that he had already dipped into his own pocket several times and, short of robbing a bank, could think of no other source of funds.)

"It's supposed to be stormy," Bren said. "We can do lightning flashes with the floods. Maybe if we lower the lights gradually and bang on the old thunder sheet more and more toward the end, we could get away with a tiny blackout."

"You'd have to have a few really quick ones during the scene," the director said, "to keep it from being too obvious, but it might work. The girls will have to be exceeding nimble."

"They are that," said Bren, who was now watching Erika's swift preparations for departure. "Excuse me, Bear." He jumped over a row of theater seats and dashed up the aisle to head Erika off at the exit.

"Can we try it tomorrow?" called Mr. Behrens, and Bren gave him an ambiguous wave of the hand.

He caught Erika at the foot of the stairs, and she turned, frowning slightly. "Hey, Erika, I'm sorry I hassled you about your hair," Bren said. "It wasn't any of my business."

She shrugged. "No problem. You know I'll do what I want anyway. Did you come dashing after me just to tell me that?"

"No, actually . . ." Bren stopped. He wondered how he had ever found her the easiest person in the world to talk to. "Actually, I had an idea of something you might like to do — with me, that is. It's awfully interesting, but maybe you'd rather not. I mean, well, suit yourself."

To his amazement, Erika laughed. "How can I suit myself if I don't even know what you want me to do?"

"Good point," Bren said. "I'd better tell you what it is."

"Right," Erika said.

"The Halloween parade in the Village," Bren said, and

when she raised her eyebrows incredulously, he plunged on. "It's not just kid stuff. They have the most wonderful costumes in the world. *Everybody* dresses up. Groups get together and build things like floating skeletons half a block long and snakes and dragons. Some of the best things they do every year, but you never know what you're going to see, and the whole Village is decorated with weird things. Everybody who wants to marches in the parade — families with kids and dogs, teen-agers, lots of grown-ups, especially the gay people from the Village. They spend the most time and come up with the best ideas. Anyway, it's amazing, and I bet you never saw anything like it."

"Okay, please stop. I'm sold, but I hate dressing up," said Erika, who spent much of her life doing just that.

"No, we'll just watch," Bren said. "I never dress up either. The crowds are horrendous, though. You're not crowd-phobic or anything?"

"I'm not crowd-phobic, and don't start trying to unconvince me. It sounds cool."

"I'll pick you up at five-thirty," Bren said. "It pays to be early, believe me. See you tomorrow." He bounded up the stairs ahead of her, reluctant to push his luck, anxious to get outside and celebrate. Halloween was only three days away, and in the interval he had to produce a convincing thunderstorm for Behrens. At the moment, all things seemed possible.

Erika stood for a moment where he had left her, bemused and delighted. Something prickly and perverse in her nature had led her to quarrel with the one person she most wanted to please, and she had found no way to reverse the downward

126

spiral of their friendship. Every time she opened her mouth to say something warm and forgiving, something snappish or sarcastic came out. Nothing in her short and lonely life had prepared her for a simple relationship.

She shrugged and laughed and started up the stairs. "Halloween!" she said to the empty stairwell. "He wants to take me out on Halloween, of all things. Well, why not?"

It was early evening when Erika reached the street. The lights of the city glowed soft and golden, seemingly full of promise for the coming night. A warm wind blew off the river. She paused in the stream of people hurrying to get home from work and thought about going home herself. It seemed a dreary prospect. If only Bren had waited, they could have walked a while together, looking in windows and making silly jokes as they had nearly every night only a short time ago. Walking by herself seemed a poor substitute, but an improvement on the apartment. Erika turned away from the Apthorp and began to walk up Broadway.

She walked north until she was tired, then crossed the street and started back toward home. By the time she was in the eighties it was almost totally dark; she was hungry, and the lonely adventure had begun to lose some of its charm. She paused in front of a coffee shop and studied its offerings. It was a small, oddly cozy-looking place with red café curtains and shaded lamps inside. Not a very Broadway place, Erika thought. Possibly it was the kind of place that put real whipped cream on hot chocolate. She went in and settled into a tiny booth. The waitress was raw-boned and motherly, like a farm woman, thought Erika, who had never been near a farm. While she waited for her chocolate, she noticed a stack of business cards on the table and examined one idly.

"Madame Rose, Spiritual Adviser," it announced, and continued in smaller print, "Madame Rose knows your future. She sees it in the magic crystal. She reads it in the stars and in the ancient Tarot cards. All questions answered. All problems clarified. Reasonable. Confidential."

Erika stared curiously at the address, which was on West Eighty-fourth Street, and then, with widening eyes, at the telephone number. The bell it rang was loud and clear. She laughed out loud, startling the pair of elderly ladies in the next booth. "Oh, Bren," she whispered. "So that's your terrible secret."

The hot chocolate came, and Erika sipped it absentmindedly, almost oblivious to it richness and plenitude of whipped cream. She was trying to remember what Bren had told her about the ladies of his household. Not his mother, she said to herself. His mother's name is Miranda, and she's young and beautiful. His grandmother, then, or the roomer in the attic. Not the black woman, although she sounds pretty weird. Oh, what a lovely secret. I'll visit Madame Rose one of these days when he's not home, if I have to cut school to do it.

Erika paid for her unappreciated chocolate and skipped out onto Broadway. She was tired no longer. The rest of the walk home seemed like nothing as she savored her new knowledge and rejoiced in the prospect of Halloween with Bren.

Chapter Fifteen

The night of Halloween would be clear and cold, much like the night of the dance program, Bren thought as he ran the few blocks from school to house. He was short of time. Eli, left alone and resentful in the theater, had insisted that he refocus one last light for the technical rehearsal the following day, and now he had to rush home to take Shadow out and pick up a warm coat to wear to the parade. It was five o'clock already, and he spared no time for his mother, who in any case was doing something in her studio with the door closed.

This shortage of time was fortunate for Bren's peace of mind. It didn't occur to him that Miranda might be dressing for the parade or that she would even think of going. Halloween was one of the two most important nights of the year for witches, and Miranda usually spent all evening in elaborate preparations for the midnight mass. Thus he was spared the ominous discovery that on this particular Halloween his mother had resolved to have a little harmless fun before settling down to the more serious business of a major Sabbat.

The streets of Greenwich Village were already filling with people when Bren and Erika arrived at six o'clock. Erika had abandoned her usual somber dress code and was wearing a huge orange ski sweater with her ankle-length black skirt. "You'll be easy to find if I lose you," Bren said.

"Just don't lose me," Erika answered. She was, in fact, a little afraid of large crowds, and Bren had promised that the sidewalks would be packed along the route of the parade.

"Don't worry," Bren said, tightening his grip on the small hand that nestled so agreeably in his own. "And now, look up!"

They had come along West Tenth Street almost to Sixth Avenue and now had a clear view of the gothic magnificence of the Jefferson Market Library. Erika stopped in her tracks, speechless with delight. The tall, pointed windows flickered with multicolored lights, and against their panes strange shapes moved and changed. There, surely, was a flight of bats, and there an evil face that peered for a moment at the crowd below and then was gone. Her eyes traveled up to the lighted clock face at the top of the tower and then down to the wrought iron balcony that encircled it. "Oh, Bren, look!"

He grinned and put his arm around her, as pleased as if he had created this wonderful set piece himself. Something was crawling over the edge of the balcony — something large and black with many groping legs, dragging its bulbous body down the side of the tower. Spotlights swept up from the dense trees behind the library and illuminated the progress of the gigantic spider creeping toward the lighted windows of the main building.

Bren gave his companion a little shake. "Come on," he said. "We've got to find a good place to stand for the parade. The spider will do its thing a lot of times tonight. Maybe we'll see him again on the way home."

They hurried through the thickening crowd to the middle

130

of the block on West Tenth. There Bren found a place at the curb directly behind a woman with three small children. "Always stand behind some little ones," he explained. "If you're at all grown up and stand in the front line, someone even more determined will come and stand in front of you, but the chances are good that no one will be mean enough to do that to a clutch of tiny tots. In this case, I think they'd better not try," he added, after getting a better look at the mother, who was wearing the traditional garb of a black belt karate expert.

Looking across the street, Erika saw why he had chosen this particular spot. The row of tall brownstones on the other side had a continuous balcony running along their parlor floors one flight up from the street, and on Halloween this balcony was used by the occupants of the houses as a natural stage. Each set of French doors stood open, and each family had contrived an appropriate tableau. Bren pointed. "Look at the Addams family."

"An obvious choice," Erika said, "but also an awful lot of work. And there's the crew of the *Enterprise* with a . . . what? . . . a chained Klingon, maybe. Bren, this is amazing. You didn't tell me."

"I might have elaborated," Bren said, "if you'd shown any sign of turning me down."

They had a long wait, but it was clear that if they had come any later, Erika would have seen nothing at all and Bren very little. The crowd behind them grew and grew. Railings, phone booths, and the lower branches of trees were draped with teen-agers, and everywhere small children bobbed on the shoulders of tall men. The atmosphere was relaxed and festive. Even the police, who made halfhearted efforts to maintain a clear path down the street, smiled and joked

131

with the people who stepped out of line. "They probably fight over who'll get this assignment," Erika commented.

The tableaux on the balcony continued to unfold, and many people in costume were already strolling down the middle of the street. At last a single police car could be seen crawling through the crowd at the corner, and the people around Bren and Erika began to applaud. No band or bannered float marked the beginning of the Halloween parade. The police car, instead, was followed by an incredibly tall man in the costume of a drum majorette. His spangled skirt came only to mid-thigh on his long and shapely legs, and the tight satin bodice clung to a seemingly perfect female form. He strode with assurance in high-heeled boots, twirling, tossing, and catching his baton. "He's beautiful," Erika said in an astonished voice, staring at the fine, aquiline features and the deep-set eyes that glanced proudly left and right at the admiring crowd.

"They all are," Bren said. "Wait till you see some of the ones in evening dresses. Oh, there's the camel. I look for him every year."

The camel was composed entirely of Oriental rugs supported by three men. This, of course, gave it six legs, but it was otherwise a quite realistic two-humped camel with a long neck and large, supercilious eyes.

Even from their vantage point, it was impossible to take in everything that went by. There were children in witch hats, cereal boxes, and sheets, often accompanied by embarrassed dogs done up in ribbons and bedraggled crepe paper. The older marchers came in bewildering variety — a chaos of inventiveness and imagination. Some of the costumes, Erika thought, must have taken the whole year to construct. She started a mental catalogue and soon lost track. There were Cleopatra, Ronald Reagan, a Valkyrie and a Sphinx, Greta Garbo and Hirohito, four coiffed and wimpled nuns with Marx Brothers faces, Tarzan, Richard Nixon, a pair of Spocks — one white-coated with a baby in his arms, the other with pointed ears — the Dalai Lama, a giant lizard with sequined scales, Red Riding Hood chased by a wolf, Theseus and the Minotaur, a bear, a woolly mammoth and Luciano Pavarotti; there were jugglers and acrobats, flamenco dancers, tap dancers, belly dancers, break dancers, and a gigantic robot whose head was a functioning television screen.

Next came the first of the enormous bands. They had been hearing it for some time, and now that it was almost upon them, Bren had to shout to be heard. "The Brazilian percussion band," he yelled. "Cover your ears, and you'll still hear it without going deaf." The band rode on linked floats pulled through the streets by enthusiastic supporters. The players were by no means all Brazilians; indeed, the entire community of New York percussionists seemed to have rallied with every kind of instrument that could conceivably be banged, thumped, or rattled. There were African drums, Caribbean drums, xylophones, ratchets, bells, snare drums, and even a set of symphony orchestra tympani. The music they made was Latin in rhythm, horrific in volume, and undeniably splendid.

In the wake of the band came a snake carried on long sticks by at least twenty people. It was half a block long and wove to and fro over the heads of the crowd, occasionally dipping its great, fanged head to snap at some half-entranced, half-terrified child.

The snake was followed by five Africans in witch doctor

costumes, striding on four-foot stilts — magnificent, terrifying, their long fringes of straw shaking, their huge, white-circled eyes staring ahead, while at their feet their own musicians danced and drummed.

After the Africans there was a gap in the parade, and this was rather a relief. It also provided a perfect stage for the next figure, who appeared alone, walking slowly and majestically down the middle of the street.

Miranda wore black from head to toe, the simple splendor of her robe broken only by a girdle of golden serpents. Her fair head was crowned with dark laurel leaves. In her right hand she carried a staff encircled by runes of power and in her left the shining, black-hilted athamé. No broom or pointed hat for Miranda, but hardly anyone in the crowd could have doubted that she was a genuine witch.

It was clear, at least to Bren, that Miranda was having a lovely time. She cast stern, piercing glances from side to side; it would be only a matter of seconds before her eyes fell upon her only son and his unsuspecting date.

"Cripes, that's the real thing," Erika muttered. At the same time Bren jerked her hand and said, "Let's get out of here. I've had enough," and made a dive for the solid wall of spectators behind them. Erika, however, had a mind of her own and had not had enough. She was fascinated by the queenly figure who was drawing abreast of them, and she gave her hand an even stronger jerk, disengaging herself from Bren, who plunged into a tiny fissure in the crowd. "Erika, come on!" he shouted, but the ranks of watchers opened and virtually sucked him in before closing again in a seamless barrier.

Thus Erika stood alone under the flashing eyes of the

black-robed queen of witches, and was astonished to see that those eyes were blue and full of mischief. The witch even smiled at her, a slightly enigmatic smile, nodded her head once up and down, and then passed on. When Erika turned to find Bren, he was gone without a trace.

Another band, this time composed of oddly assorted wind instruments, was coming down the street playing ragtime. The crowd began to sway and sing, and Erika felt the first small wave of panic wash over her. He'll come back for me, she said to herself. Or will he? She studied the mob behind her. It was clear that wanting to come back for her and being able to were not the same thing. "I've got to get out of here," Erika said out loud, but nobody heard her. She could hardly hear herself. The people who hemmed her in were still a cheerful, happy lot, but their grinning faces began to take on a look of manic mindlessness that was almost as frightening as hostility.

"Excuse me!" Erika shouted at the huge man who stood behind her. It was like yelling at the Empire State Building. Her head reached only to the middle button on his red hunting jacket, and he was craning his neck to see the band. Erika, now quite desperate, stamped ferociously with one high-heeled boot on his sneakered toe and was momentarily pleased with the effect. He howled and staggered back into the crowd. The resulting turbulence permitted her to squeeze through as far as the iron railings that separated the houses from the sidewalk. Here her situation was hardly improved, but she was angry now as well as frightened. Slowly, painfully, twisting, squirming, and occasionally stamping, she made her way to the corner of Sixth Avenue and burst out of the crowd into open space.

Chapter Sixteen

Erika was disoriented. She had paid little attention to the route she had followed a few hours before with Bren — Bren the comforting and knowledgeable New Yorker who had abandoned her in this nightmarish mob scene. It was clear that she was not going to find him again except by some extraordinary stroke of good luck, and Erika felt that her luck had definitely run out. She would have to go home alone, and that meant finding the subway. To her left across Sixth Avenue the eerie Jefferson Market tower stood against the black sky. The spider was climbing up to its balcony, while the lower windows flickered ominously. "That's where it is, then," Erika said aloud, "and it's only a few blocks away." She crossed the avenue, but the street she thought they had taken was choked by the parade. I'll just make a small circle to the left, Erika thought, and come out at the Christopher Street station.

It was a reasonable strategy, but not one recommended to a stranger in the Village. She walked through unfamiliar streets, buffeted by indifferent merrymakers, increasingly confused and disheartened. I'm lost, she said to herself, hopelessly and ridiculously lost. And now the feeling of being physically lost expanded and grew into a sense of general loss, of a desolation so sharp that it made her catch her breath in a gasp of pain. Why had Bren left her when he had seemed so eager for their date, so enchanted with her company? Once, when she was just starting junior high, an older boy had asked her to meet him in front of a theater where a wonderful rock group was to play. She had taken hours to dress and had escaped the house by elaborate subterfuge, only to stand for an hour trying to look casual and sophisticated while a throng of teen-agers jostled their way into the theater. Later she learned that she had been stood up for a joke.

But I hardly knew that jerk, she thought. This was different. This was Bren, the original sweetheart who wouldn't be rude to a roach. Miserable though she was, Erika felt sure there was no kinship between Bren and the sadistic prankster of her twelfth year, but the painful memory reinforced the loneliness and confusion of the present. "They're all alike," she muttered. "Creeps, rat finks. But this won't get me home, and home is where I truly want to be."

Erika looked around for someone to ask the way to the subway, but found it difficult to address Miss Piggy and the Phantom of the Opera, who were coming down the sidewalk with their arms around each other. She leaned against the trunk of a tree, thinking that perhaps, if she just stood still for a moment, sanity and some sense of direction would return. Instead there was a hoarse animal cry above her head, followed by a great rustling and cracking of branches. She looked up and stifled a scream as an enormous gorilla dropped to the sidewalk at her feet. "Ha! Little white woman," the gorilla snarled. "Now I have you in my power." The sight was horrific, but the voice was familiar.

"Jeremy!" Erika cried. "God, you scared me, but am I glad to hear a familiar voice. I am utterly lost in this stupid part of town. Nothing makes any sense."

"You come down here alone?" asked the gorilla. "That's a mistake for a foreigner."

"I actually came with Bren," Erika said, but some remnant of loyalty made her add, "We got separated somehow, and there's no way you can find anybody again. I can't even find the subway. I've been trying for hours."

"Good old Bren," Jeremy said. "He sure has a talent for screwing things up. Did you get to see the parade?"

"Some of it — a lot of it, I guess. It was awesome. I wouldn't have missed it, but right now the dear old boring comforts of home are looking very good. Where's the subway, Jeremy? I know it can't be far, but I could wander around here for the rest of my life without finding it."

The gorilla dug into the fur around its stomach and produced a large pocket watch. "Can't go home at nine o'clock on Halloween," it said. "Let's party."

Erika was beginning to feel disoriented again. "Party?" she asked. "Here?"

"Village is full of parties. Full of subways, too, so don't worry. Come on."

Erika found her wrist imprisoned in a hairy paw and was dragged protesting down the street. "I don't have a costume. I don't feel festive," she began, but it was even harder to talk to the back of a gorilla's head than to Miss Piggy and the

Phantom. She gave up and yielded to the persistent pull of the creature she knew to be Jeremy.

They turned into the doorway of a small, shabby apartment building and began to climb the stairs. Disco music grew louder with each of the five flights. The door at the top stood open, and Erika saw what appeared to be an impenetrable mass of bodies writhing and swaying under a revolving light that illuminated the costumed dancers in a succession of garish colors — red, purple, orange, green. Jeremy seemed to know the place, however, and she followed him willingly now as he wormed his way around the mob to a small open space where a formidable stack of warm Budweiser cans stood on a rickety table.

Erika accepted the unappetizing beverage gratefully and gulped it down. "Thirsty," she commented to Jeremy, who did not reply. It was disconcerting to be with someone whose features were so completely masked. Jeremy's face might be expressing admiration, disgust, boredom, lechery, or a host of other emotions as he watched her drink; all she could see was the conventional snarl of animal rage beneath the gorilla's beetling brows. She looked around the room, which seemed to be unfurnished except for the table and some large pillows pushed into corners. On one of these, an athletic-looking girl, wearing copper arm bands, a stuffed boa constrictor, and little else, grappled enthusiastically with Darth Vader. The latter was impeded by his elaborate costume, which he seemed to be trying to shed. Erika looked away and saw the first of several supplementary lighting fixtures. Cleverly constructed of translucent plastic, it was all too obviously a severed leg streaked realistically with gore.

"The rest of the body is scattered around," Jeremy said, following her gaze. "They do it every year."

"Less than tasteful," Erika commented, taking another beer.

"You think so?" Jeremy sounded puzzled. "I thought it was neat."

"You would," Erika said, then added more charitably, "That stuff would make great props, I guess."

"Yeah. Wait till you see the head. It's a prop man's dream."

"I'll pass," Erika said. "Let's dance." She backed into the wriggling throng and soon lost Jeremy. No one seemed to have a partner anyway. At least it would have been hard to tell which costumed figure belonged to which. With the overpowering music and the warm beer beating in her veins, Erika began, briefly, to enjoy herself.

First one bizarre male figure and then another bounded into the small space in front of her, grinning, jerking, undulating, gyrating. There was an energetic fat boy in a space suit; then a coal miner streaked with sweat and soot (no close dancing with this one, Erika thought); then another gorilla, brown this time, so it wasn't Jeremy. "What's with the gorillas this year?" Erika shouted, but wasn't heard in the horrendous din. She was overheating badly in her orange ski sweater, and there really wasn't room to dance. As her enthusiasm flagged, the whole scene took on a nightmarish quality. A huge black man, who might have come straight from the witch doctor act in the parade, leapt in front of her previous partner. He was almost naked except for a grass skirt, a headdress, and much vivid body paint. There seemed to be a bone thrust through his nostrils. "This is carrying the fun of make-believe a bit far," Erika said, confident that he couldn't hear a word. Certainly he was an amazing dancer, and she thought how, in more favorable conditions, she might have enjoyed trying to imitate the boneless twisting of his shining, paint-streaked torso, his stupendous leaps into the air. Instead she felt suddenly exhausted, awkward, and incompetent in her heavy, unsuitable clothes.

She was rescued by Jeremy, her black gorilla, who had finally managed to reach her through the crush. Jeremy, apparently, was no dancer. He grabbed her wrist and pulled her from the dance floor and around a corner into a narrow hall.

"Sorry," Erika said, as soon as she could be heard. "I thought you wanted to dance."

"Did you ask?" Jeremy inquired.

"I just sort of got sucked in," Erika said. "Anyway, it wasn't much fun, and here I am!" She felt vaguely that she owed Jeremy something.

He seemed to think so too. He pulled off the entire head of his costume and stood grinning at her, his handsome face and blond hair rising incongruously from shaggy black shoulders. "There's all kinds of fun," said Jeremy, advancing upon her.

Erika retreated to a corner of the hall and stopped. "Just don't carry me off, Godzilla," she said. She was fighting a sense of futility, a feeling of déjà vu. It was true she had never been mauled by a gorilla with a human head before, but otherwise this end-of-party scene was depressingly familiar. Jeremy's furry embrace was hot and prickly, his kisses experienced but lacking in finesse. Erika made a heroic effort, but then she thought of Bren in the cool morning by the river. It wouldn't do. She tried a polite withdrawal, knowing full well that there is no such thing.

"I'm just awfully hot and tired," she said. "I'm sorry, Jeremy. You were sweet to bring me here. I knew I should have gone home, and now I've got to."

"Well, hot you're not," Jeremy said disgustedly. "I sure guessed wrong about that. Now I suppose you want me to take you to the subway and miss some more of this great party."

"I'll find it myself, thanks," Erika said.

"Just go right at the door and then right again. Even you can't miss it." Jeremy was peering into the living room, where a girl in a beaded chemise that ended less than an inch below her crotch was lighting a cigarette in a long holder.

Erika wasted no more time on apologies. It was a battle to get out of the apartment, but one she was glad to fight. The crowd was even denser, the noise level even more appalling. "Did I use to like this sort of thing?" she mumbled. "Surely not!"

The street was cold, littered, and nearly deserted. "Heavenly," said Erika, and headed for the subway, which she found without delay.

An hour earlier Bren had taken the uptown train from Sheridan Square. The journey to Eighty-sixth Street, amid crowds of tired children being taken home by parents and exuberant teen-agers whose night was still young, had been grim and interminable.

He had stalked the edges of the parade in a rage, blaming first his mother for her juvenile notion of Halloween fun and then himself for not sticking to Erika at all costs. The likelihood that Miranda would have greeted him or revealed their relationship was small, and surely anything would have been better than this horrible conclusion to what had seemed so promising an evening. This has to be the end, he thought as he climbed the subway stairs, and it is all, one hundred percent, my fault. What's worse, I have to call her and see if she got home all right. Bren cast about for a plausible reason for abandoning his date in the middle of the Halloween parade. Short of some kind of fit or psychic breakdown, he could think of nothing remotely believable, and there had already been the hideous incident of the supposed migraine headache after the dance program. "I ought to be put away in a loony bin," he muttered, momentarily forgetting that these excuses were entirely of his own invention.

All three witches having gone to separate Sabbats, the house was empty when Bren arrived. He went to the phone bravely, like a martyr to the stake, but there was no answer from the Apthorp. What if she's lost down there, he thought, or something worse? The Village is full of creeps. I've not only made her mad, I've endangered her life. He paced the kitchen floor, circling the couch and ignoring Shadow, who was baffled and hurt. Passing the mantel for the third time, his eye fell upon the bottle of Scotch Miranda kept for his father. "I'll get drunk," he said, seizing the bottle and turning suddenly on his startled dog. "That's what people do when they can't cope."

An abstemious life of beer and the occasional margarita had not prepared Bren for straight whisky, but in spite of the awful taste, he persevered. He put the bottle beside the telephone, pulled up a chair, and began a siege of dialing interspersed with determined gulps of Scotch. Time went by, and the sound of the telephone ringing in an empty apartment came to seem normal to his increasingly muddled brain. When Erika answered, he almost dropped the bottle.

"Erika!" he shouted. "Where are you?"

"Where do you think I am, lamebrain?" she snapped.

"I don't mean where are you. I mean *how* are you?" Bren said wildly. "I mean are you all right? I've been going crazy."

"Going crazy?" Erika said. "How far did you have to go?"

"You're right," he said. "It was crazy to go off and leave you like that."

"Then why did you do it?"

"I don't know," Bren cried. "I'm sorry, I just don't know, but I was horribly worried about you. It's taken you hours to get home."

"Oh, that was no problem." Erika's voice had grown cool and airy. "I met Jeremy. Isn't that amazing? He was wearing the most awesome gorilla suit, and he took me to this really neat party. I had a lovely time."

"You've been out with Jeremy all this time?" Bren yelled into the phone. "Why didn't you call me?"

"Frankly, the thought never entered my head," she replied. "Why would it? You know, you really don't sound normal."

"I'm drunk," Bren said. "Drunk as a skunk. That's an old saying."

"Picturesque, but I think I've heard it before," Erika said.

Alcohol, frustration, and guilt produced in Bren an emotion that was strange to him; he was totally and irrationally enraged.

"Picturesque," he snarled. "Always the neat, smart word.

Always calm, cool, and collected. You know what I think? I think something got left out of you. I don't think you've got a scrap of feeling anywhere."

"Maybe if you stuck around once in a while, you'd find out," Erika said.

There was a brief silence. Bren felt anger drain away, to be replaced by an immense hopelessness. "I did once," he said, "or twice, really. The second time didn't do me any good."

"Too bad you won't get another chance," Erika said, and hung up the phone.

Bren sat looking at the dead thing which was the telephone receiver as if uncertain of its use. Shadow put a heavy paw on his knee and whined. "Well, that's that," he said to the dog. "We're going to have to backtrack, old boy, and find out what made life so wonderful before she came along with her little silver monkey wrench." This conceit pleased him for a moment. He thought about going to bed and beginning a new, monkish life in the morning; but then he remembered that morning meant an all-day technical rehearsal, and he groaned. How, hung over, short of sleep, and deprived forever of Erika, was he going to survive such an ordeal?

"We won't even get to go to the park," he said to Shadow as he stumbled to his feet, "but come on. At least we can sleep together."

Chapter Seventeen

"I shall unseam you from the navel to the chops," shouted Edward Behrens. "I'll fix your head upon my battlements."

He stood in the first row of the theater and glared up at his Macbeth, an imposing figure, kilted and cloaked in dark plaids but wearing the petulant expression of an exhausted child.

The rehearsal had begun well, with the three stunningly repulsive witches chanting, "When shall we three meet again, in thunder, lightning, or in rain?" It had foundered eleven lines later as the king, a sturdy scholarship student from the Bronx, entered with his soldiers and demanded, "What bloody man is that?" Not everyone in the company had heard this treacherous line before, and those who had not infected those who had with their unseemly mirth. Once order had been restored, Behrens's patience was tried again as Bren and the sound man struggled to produce a gradually increasing thunderstorm during the second appearance of the witches. Lightning flashed and thunder rolled, but never at appropriate times, and often the thunder came before the lightning, as if Bren had to be reminded to flash the flood-lights. The blackout had to be done a dozen times before the girls managed to vanish without a trace. Would it work on opening night? Probably not, the director thought, but technical problems were the reason for having technical rehearsals. Ego tantrums were not.

"Please tell me, Brian," he continued in a dangerously calm voice, "why, when we have spent endless weeks blocking this misbegotten play, you insist upon delivering every line downstage center with your back to the other characters."

"It doesn't feel right to go upstage on that line," the actor said.

"It doesn't *feel* right?" Behrens repeated. "Now he says it doesn't feel right. In the first place, you have done it properly a hundred times before. In the second place, this is a *tech* rehearsal, Brian. This is not a feeling rehearsal, except for my feelings, which are at the moment just short of savage."

Brian smirked and seized his advantage. "All right, then, it's dark up there," he said, pointing at the spot some six feet behind him where his Lady stood, tapping her foot.

With a sigh of resignation, Behrens turned toward the light booth. "Eli, just a shade brighter upstage right for Laurence Olivier here, and then maybe we can get on with it before we all die of old age."

At the switchboard Eli groaned, turned a dial, and scribbled furiously on his clipboard.

"That's thrown everything else out of balance," Bren observed, peering down at the stage.

"Please," Eli said. "Do me a favor, Bren."

"What?"

"Two favors. One, don't make any remarks. Two, get me another Coke."

"Yes, master," Bren said, and headed for the Coke machine while the play lurched forward a few more lines and stopped again.

The second and third witches were also buying Cokes. He supposed the first was avoiding him, but from the prison of the light booth it had been hard to tell.

The second witch was a tall, bony girl whose blond hair, powdered gray, hung in lank strands against her ravaged cheeks. Polly, the third witch, was normally plump and cheerful. She had never seemed really fat, but for *Macbeth* she had contrived the look of a monstrous, nocturnal toad — bloated, pale, and evil-looking. They were dressed in scanty rags over leotards the same color as their pale gray skins. They had black lips and wispy beards and were gossiping about a party.

"Hail, lovely ladies," Bren said, feeding his coins into the Coke machine. "When, think you, comes an end to this ghastly day?"

"Hail, good McBren," said Polly, and then they chanted together, " 'When the hurlyburly's done, When the battle's lost and won.' But," finished the tall witch, "that won't be ere the set of sun, unless the Bear murders the Rushmore and plays Macbeth himself."

"I think the sun set hours ago," Bren said, "but you can't tell in this tomb."

The rehearsal had started at two o'clock and had so far progressed to Act Two, Scene One. Soon sandwiches would be brought in, after which cast and crew would struggle on into the night. With weekday curfews and schoolwork in mind, Mr. Behrens had decided to hold the first technical on Saturday and the second technical and the dress rehearsal the Wednesday and Thursday nights before the Friday opening. He knew that the interval might prove disastrous, but he had been even more reluctant to keep everyone up all night during the week.

"How do we look?" Polly asked, doing an exaggerated model's turn, her fat jiggling, her bearded chin tipped up at a provocative angle. "I wish we could see ourselves from out front. Someone simply has to take pictures."

"Utterly ravishing," Bren said, then added casually, "but where's the third weird sister?"

"She's in a sulk tonight," Polly confided. "Sits in a corner with a book except when Jeremy wants her for something."

Bren felt a thud in the pit of his stomach. Why had he asked? Even though he felt terrible, and his lighting earlier in the play had been a disaster, some of the despair of the night before had lifted. Now it settled again like a black mist.

"When Jeremy wants her for something," he repeated dully.

"You know, to hand him props or whatever," Polly amplified.

But Bren refused to be reassured. He pictured Erika and Jeremy backstage. They would be joking in whispers, chuckling and nudging each other. In the dark alleys between the masking curtains, they would wait for their cues and kiss. He had seen her only from afar as she played the first witch scenes at the beginning of the play, noting that her costume and makeup, enhanced by sharp spikes of shocking pink hair, were even more gruesomely effective than those of the other two.

"I'd better take Eli his Coke," he said, "before he collapses on the switchboard and electrocutes himself."

"I'll tell Erika you asked about her," Polly said with a knowing smile.

149

"Thanks, Pol. I'm sure that will be riveting news," Bren said, and retreated toward the sanctuary of the light booth. As he crossed the back of the house, he was appalled to see that the rehearsal had taken a leap forward and almost reached another of his scenes.

"Great timing," Eli said, sliding out of his seat as Bren charged into the light booth. "Don't get rattled. You've got at least thirty seconds to find your place."

Thirty seconds was not enough. The coming scene, in which Macduff discovers the body of the murdered king, was Bren's pride and joy. Its effects were subtle, complex, and terrifyingly beautiful. The cue arrived, and he was still frantically searching the lighting script.

When the sequence failed to begin, Behrens stopped the rehearsal. "Are you geniuses asleep up there?" he shouted.

"I've got it now," Bren called. "Sorry." But he was still fumbling.

Eli leaned over his shoulder and started the cue. "Pull yourself together," he hissed. "This thing has to be done right. If you can't do it, I will."

"I can do it. I just got lost. Why am I the only one who's not allowed to screw up?" Bren asked.

"You've been screwing up all day," Eli said, and continued to work the lights.

Bren scrunched miserably in his seat as Eli took over his cues, not only from the murder, but all the way through the dispatching of Banquo on the heath. He had not only missed his favorite scene, he missed his last scene before the final appearance of the witches.

Soon they would break for sandwiches. I'll go out to a deli, Bren thought, and wander around on Broadway. Even this seemed better than a convivial gathering of actors and technicians, during which he would surely have to watch Jeremy and Erika flirting while they ate. He had not spoken to her since the horrible telephone conversation of the night before, but it seemed pointless even to try. When the break came, he went straight out to the street without going down into the theater, thus avoiding Behrens as well as Erika.

After a lonely sandwich on Broadway, the evening still stretched interminably ahead. "I could have gone home and had a nap," Bren grumbled to himself as he waited in the light booth while the play crawled forward. But Eli might need him to refocus a light or change a gel. A technical rehearsal involves not only major crises, but innumerable small changes in costumes, makeup, props, and lights.

The final witch scene with its projected apparitions called for the efforts of both light men, and technically it went quite well. Eli appeared to have forgotten his earlier impatience, and in any case he could not have managed alone. Bren was determined not to disgrace himself again. He watched the witches almost without interest except for the lines and movements that were cues to change the lights. Even so, he could hardly fail to notice that their performance was very poor. Erika in particular had lost her edge. She seemed dispirited, and her timing was off. Several times she stumbled, and her awkwardness confused the other two, who had come to depend upon her leadership.

Down in the house, Edward Behrens sighed, took notes, and let it pass. He still had the fight and the coming of Birnam Wood to Dunsinane ahead of him; a little lousy dancing could be overlooked. But during the following scene he felt a small thump in the next seat and turned to see Erika beside him. Even in the dim light that spilled from the stage, he could see streaks of tears in her horrible gray makeup. She gave her beard a vicious yank, and most of it came off in her hand.

"It'll come right," Behrens whispered to his favorite witch.

She shook her head. "I blew it, and I'm going to blow it again," she muttered.

"You won't, you know. This is just tech rehearsal blues."

"I wish it were," Erika said. "I'm afraid it's something much, much worse."

Behrens reached out to give her spiky head a reassuring pat, then leapt to his feet as he saw the scene onstage end in unparalleled confusion. The wife of Ross, hotly pursued by a murderer, had caught her foot on a strut projecting from the tower of her castle. This began slowly to revolve and then to break apart as Jeremy plunged onto the stage, both hands outstretched in a futile effort to hold it up.

"The devil damn thee black, thou cream-faced loon!" the director cried, and from their various stations around the theater, the entire cast and crew broke into gales of wild hilarity.

The remainder of the rehearsal was an anticlimax. The burst of laughter seemed to have done everyone good, and the company slogged through the rest of the play, changed into street clothes, and went gratefully home.

Only Eli remained to fiddle with a single spotlight on the edge of the balcony. Behrens watched him for a moment before turning wearily to climb the stairs. He would have to say something about the lights, for which he had felt such confident expectations. He knew that Eli had replaced Bren in the scenes before the intermission, and it now seemed to

152

him that he had been a fool to entrust such a vital task to anyone so inexperienced.

"I feel mean as a dog," he said to Eli when he had joined him at the balcony rail, "but I think you're going to have to take over the things Bren was doing by himself. We can run them through one extra time to give you the practice."

Surprisingly, Eli shook his head. "He'll be all right," he said. "Leave him alone, if you can stand it."

"I don't know how much more I can stand," Behrens said. "His work was an almost total disaster tonight, and it's not as if it weren't really crucial stuff. I'm sure you thought you knew what you were doing, but he'd never even seen a light board before this play, right?"

"That's right," Eli said, "but he's really good. He's got a fantastic touch for it. Just something was wrong tonight. He was sick or something. Trust me, Bear. We've got almost a week for him to get over whatever it is, and two more rehearsals."

The director was silent, studying the skinny, tireless boy bent over the spotlight. Then he shrugged. "Well, I guess you're right, however it turns out," he said. "After all, this is supposed to be an educational institution, not the Royal Shakespeare Company. Give him some aspirin and a kick in the ass, and we'll hope for the best."

"And the best is what you'll get," Eli said with a grin, and went back to the light booth to turn off the spot and put the board to bed for the night. Soon he too was gone, and Edward Behrens was left alone in his dimly lit theater.

At least he should have been alone, since all the cast and crew had departed, but as soon as he reached the back of the house, he had a strong sensation that he was being watched. This part of the theater, which had been dark during the rehearsal, was now faintly illuminated by wall sconces turned low. He was being watched, and now he was being addressed from the shadowy corner under the balcony to his left.

"Hello, poor, tired Bear," said the voice, which was female and quite beautiful. "I wish I had some honey to give you, but sympathy is all I have to offer."

Behrens whirled and saw the tall woman who sat, relaxed and smiling, at the far end of the back row. She had a black scarf over her head which now she pulled off, releasing a cloud of bright hair. "Miranda West," she said, holding out a slim hand. "Come sit by my side and tell me all your woes."

Behrens's first reaction had been one of outrage that some stranger had sat there for God only knew how long watching the horrible floundering of his rehearsal. Now, as he leaned over the row of seats and took the proffered hand, he was not sure it was such a bad thing after all. Bren's mother was certainly an astonishingly attractive woman, and he found himself thinking that he had spent not only the past weeks but several centuries in the exclusive company of high school students.

Miranda moved over and pointed invitingly to the place at the end of the row. Behrens sat down. He found himself wondering whether Bren had a father and inhaling a faint, unfamiliar, but curiously intoxicating perfume. Even in the gloom at the back of the theater, the woman's eyes were disturbingly blue. Her smile was at once mischievous and friendly. The impulse to tell her everything about himself was almost irresistible, but not quite. Sophisticated and la-

154

conic, he said to himself. That's what you want to be at a time like this.

"All my woes," he asked, "or only those occasioned by this wretched play?"

"We could start with the play," Miranda suggested, "and work backward."

"Do you have all night, then?"

"I don't see why not," she said, and settled back in her chair.

Behrens laughed. "No, really. You don't want to hear it. The feelings one has after a technical rehearsal are better left unexpressed, since they are bound to be greatly exaggerated and mostly suicidal. It will all look better in the morning."

His companion seemed genuinely surprised. "I thought it went remarkably well," she said. "What's a little falling scenery and a missed light cue or two? They won't happen again."

"You're probably right that the same things won't happen again," he said. "It's the things just like them that are waiting to happen. It's the disease, not the symptoms. The damn play is just not ready, and I have no one to blame but myself."

"Nonsense," Miranda said briskly. "Anyone can see that you have done a marvelous job against frightful odds. *Macbeth* is not the easiest play in the world, you know."

"I don't know what possessed me to choose it."

"You can't be the first person to ask himself that question," she said, "but it has a fatal fascination. Even the fact that it carries a curse doesn't seem to discourage people from producing it. Rather the contrary, I suspect."

"A curse?" Behrens said. "That's all I need."

Miranda's eyes widened, and she leaned toward him, studying his face intently. "I can't believe you didn't know about the curse of *Macbeth*. If I'd had any idea, I wouldn't have mentioned it, but maybe it's just as well I did. You've still got almost a week to straighten things out with the dark powers."

"Lovely lady," Behrens said. "I don't know what the hell you're talking about, but I do know that if this play is cursed, it's cursed by incompetence and nothing more mysterious than that."

"I suppose you've been going around saying '*Macbeth*' all the time," Miranda continued, as if he hadn't spoken. "I suppose you say things like, 'Now we'll take Scene One of *Macbeth*,' or '*Macbeth* is a difficult play for young people,' or 'The lighting for *Macbeth* is a challenge,' don't you?"

"It seems more than likely that I do," Behrens said dryly. "What am I supposed to say?"

"People call it 'the Scottish play,'" Miranda explained, "or, I suppose, just 'the play,' if they are actually in it, but never '*Macbeth*.'"

"Does this curious proscription apply to mentions of Macbeth in the script?" the director asked.

"Of course not. Don't be silly."

"Silly! Who's being silly?"

"Not I, I promise you," Miranda said with a satisfied little smile. "You see, I know about these things. But maybe it's not too late. If you will just watch your tongue for the next few days, all may yet be well."

"I'd rather watch my kids," Behrens said. "I'm trying to figure out why the lousy ones are improving and the terrific ones are going all to pot. The first witch, for example, a fantastically talented girl who was lifting those scenes right up into the realm of art, and now she's tripping over her own feet. And your son, not to mince words. I thought I had found a new genius in stage lighting, and tonight he couldn't even find his place in the script."

Miranda looked thoughtful. "Of course, it's complicated," she said after a pause. "It might be the curse, and then again, it might be love. I'm not sure which is worse. Probably it's both, and if it is, you're going to need a lot of help, Edward Bear."

"Love!" he said. "Curses. What I need is more rehearsal time."

"Time may do wonders for the torments of the heart," Miranda said, "or make them worse. Only an expert can lift a curse."

Behrens was beginning to feel that enchanting though his new friend might be, she was surely a little mad. It was not a quality he felt prepared to cope with at the moment. He rose from his seat. "Well, lacking an expert," he said, "and since I can't possibly remember not to say the name of my play for a week, perhaps you'll pray for me."

"Would you really like me to?" There was no mistaking the eagerness in her voice.

"It can't do any harm," said Behrens, extending his hand.

She pressed his fingers lightly, and he felt a tingling wave pass up his arm, through the base of his neck, and into his brain.

"I'll give it my most serious attention," said Miranda West, and, following him up the stairs and out into the street, she turned toward the river and vanished into the night without another word.

157

Chapter Eighteen

During the next four days, only Miranda could have been said to be on top of the world. She felt extraordinarily well — younger, more beautiful and, to her intense satisfaction, more powerful than she could ever remember. Perhaps it was the renewal of the great Sabbat of Halloween, the witches' New Year, when the tides of darkness turn to flood, and the rest of the world shrinks from the prophetic gales of November; but there were other things to make her happy.

Boredom had driven her to attend the technical rehearsal of *Macbeth*, and her impulse had been well rewarded. She had met an attractive man and had begun to see the vague outlines of a fascinating professional challenge. Her promise to Behrens that she would pray for him had been both playful and extremely general. She had, in fact, not the slightest idea how to lift the curse from *Macbeth* if, indeed, it was cursed at all. Miranda was a serious witch and not impressed by most old wives' tales. In her opinion, if a play was going to be cursed, it would have to be cursed by someone who knew the ropes. Whatever an innocent like Behrens might say or fail to say would surely have little influence on the princely powers she could command.

On the other hand, the play certainly appeared to be in trouble. What more agreeable task could there be than to work some potent magic for the improvement of *Macbeth* and to please a well-favored, single male at the same time? Only the method remained to be discovered. Miranda studied the script in the privacy of her tower and tried to question Bren, who was sullen and withdrawn. Still, though no plan came immediately to mind, she was not discouraged. It was good to have a major project in hand, and besides she had received a piece of news that gave an added boost to her spirits.

Alia was sick. Bren had discovered this on Sunday when he called to invite his father to the opening of *Macbeth*. "Mom is coming too, of course," he said. He was standing in the empty kitchen, one ear cocked for his mother's light step in the hall. "So maybe if Alia didn't . . ."

"I wasn't born yesterday, Bren." His father sounded tired and irritable. "Besides, she's not well — won't go anywhere or do anything. I feel sorry for her, but it's no fun. She just mopes and carries on about odd aches and pains."

"Some sort of low-level flu?" Bren suggested.

"Something like that. Anyway, it's boring. I'll be glad to see your play and even your mother's always invigorating face."

Bren was cheered by this report of Alia's malaise, and Miranda was transported. Witches are supposed to have perfect confidence in their powers. Without assurance, without what amounts to an act of faith, the most ancient and elaborate spell stands not a chance of success. Still, as Miranda said, it's always nice to have some positive feedback.

Bren enjoyed the affection and prestige that fall to the bringer of glad tidings and went back to brooding over Erika.

The need to construct a whole new tower and reinforce the rest of the scenery against a repetition of Saturday's catastrophe kept Erika busy but not amused. She was tired of stage carpentry, of bent nails and mashed fingers and the gluey smell of stage paint, and she was monumentally tired of Jeremy.

"He might as well wear a gorilla suit all year round," she grumbled to Polly, who was patiently holding up one side of the tower while Erika banged on the other. "All he talks about is sizing and two–by–fours. Ouch! Damn! I can't seem to hit a nail anymore, and I should be practicing. I get worse every day."

"You practice too much. Just let it go now, and it'll turn out great."

Erika gave the trembling structure a savage wallop. "I wish everyone would stop telling me that when I know better."

"But it's true," Polly said. "Even the Bear says we should relax and turn it all over to our subconscious minds."

"The subconscious mind never did anything for a dancer's legs, so far as I know."

"Oh, stop it. Go find Bren and tell him you're sorry or whatever he wants to be told." Polly stepped back with an exasperated gesture, and the tower swayed ominously.

"I'm not sorry. I haven't got anything to be sorry for. Hold on, dimwit! This thing isn't braced yet."

"Don't get riled," Polly said, rescuing the wavering construction, "but hurry up. This is terminal boredom, my dear."

"Riled," Erika muttered, going backstage for another handful of nails. "Riled. If that were even the half of it."

On her way home that Monday night in the chill November wind, Erika thrust her hands deep into her jacket pockets and found a tattered cardboard rectangle. She stopped under a street light and gazed long and hard at the neat calligraphy.

The unhappy night of Halloween followed by the horrible technical rehearsal had driven her curiosity about Madame Rose into the back of her mind. Now, in spite of her disillusionment with Bren, it began to smolder again. "What difference does it make?" she said angrily. "So his grandmother's a fortuneteller. She could have two heads for all I care."

Still, the teasing sensation would not go away. She wanted to know about the house from which she had been so mysteriously excluded; and, without knowing why, she felt sure that whatever was hidden on West Eighty-fourth Street was the key to her present misery. Pretending she didn't care was all very well, but it didn't seem to be getting her anywhere. Far from putting Bren out of her mind, Erika had felt a pang of grief every time the lights changed during the rehearsal, every time she tripped over a cable, every time someone referred in the most casual way to the distant and largely unseen occupants of the light booth.

Erika stuffed the card back into her pocket and turned toward home. Well, I'll do it, she said to herself. Why not? I'll visit this bogus old lady, and it will turn out to be sordid and stupid and have nothing to do with me and Bren, and that will be the end of it. This made Erika feel better. Taking some action seemed preferable to hours of brooding stretching ahead into an infinite, gray future.

It was Wednesday before she managed to gather sufficient courage to cut her afternoon classes and set out for a consultation with Madame Rose.

It was a dramatic day, alternately bright and dark, as wind-driven clouds fled across the face of the sun. When she reached the house, the light shone full on the high stoop and dark paneled door. Erika ran up the steps in a burst of optimism, which was quenched a moment later as the sun disappeared again and she stood listening to the bell ring in the depths of the house.

At last the door was opened by a plump old lady with rosy cheeks and a malevolent eye. "No Girl Scout cookies," she said angrily, "and if you've come for a consultation, you should have called."

"I'm sorry," Erika said. "It was sort of a spur-of-the-moment inspiration, and no, I'm not selling cookies or anything else. I found your card in my pocket, and I thought, well, why not?" She gave Rose her best silvery smile.

There was a crash at the back of the hall as Shadow, roused by their voices, knocked over the umbrella stand in his haste to greet an old friend. He'd give me away if he could speak, thought Erika, bending a disapproving look on the capering dog. "Don't mind him," Rose said. "He thinks he owns the place. I suppose you might as well come in. I'm not busy, as it happens, but call next time."

"I will," Erika promised, as she followed the fortuneteller into the front parlor. Bren's living room, she thought, but there was nothing of Bren in the dim, Victorian interior. The

162

windows were shrouded with heavy swags of silk, and she could barely make out the crouching shapes of horsehair sofa and rolltop desk. Then the old lady pulled the chain of a hanging lamp, and she saw the table draped in black with the great crystal glowing in the center of a white triangle.

"Cards or crystal?" snapped Madame Rose. "Ten dollars either way; both for eighteen. Pay in advance."

Erika dug in her pocket. "Just the crystal, please," she said, handing over a ten-dollar bill.

"They all want the crystal," Rose grumbled. "All the young ones. Cards tell you more, but the crystal looks more magical, so that's what they want. Sit over there and be quiet."

Erika obeyed and perched on the edge of a chair across from the fortuneteller, who was regarding her intently with bright and not altogether hostile eyes. She was already quite speechless with apprehension, and the shimmering presence of the crystal was affecting her strangely. She could feel the blood thumping in her head and her breath quickening.

Rose broke the silence. "I suppose it's a boyfriend, isn't it? Always boyfriends. Always the same old questions. Who does he love? Who's he going to marry? You're a little young for that, if you ask me."

"Not at all," Erika said indignantly. "I mean, that's not the only thing I'm interested in."

Now Rose shifted her penetrating gaze from Erika's face to the rest of Erika, and her eyes brightened slightly. "Something else, is it? It's boys, but it's something else too. Career. Success. You're an artist of some kind. A *failed* artist, or so you think in the dark days of your sixteenth year. You thought you were God's gift to the dance, and now you think you're God's greatest fool. Aha! I've got you this time."

Erika felt her face grow hot, then cold again, but she didn't answer. Madame Rose seemed to approve. "Good," she said. "Don't say a word. Vassago is a mighty prince, so don't ask any stupid questions. The crystal shows what he wants us to know, and it might be about bees or elephants as easily as love or success. Here. Write down everything I see." She handed her startled subject a pad and pencil and turned out the light.

Erika sat in the gloom and felt her scalp prickle. She had come to find out about Bren, chiefly by prying into the secrets of his house, but now she felt she had been launched on a voyage into a supernatural world she had never even believed in. A match flared as Rose lit the two tall white candles on either side of the crystal. She muttered something under her breath and made the sign of the cross three times in the air before seating herself to gaze into the fire-flecked depths.

Silence fell about them like a shroud, shutting away the sounds of the street beyond the heavy curtains and the curious snuffling of the dog in the hall. After what could have been a minute or an hour, the voice of the visionary came again, soft and remote and deeply respectful. "He is here," it said. "Vassago is here," and Erika felt a chill go down her spine.

"I am in a cave," the voice went on. "There are strange implements on the floor. I see them well, although it is utterly dark. A spoon, a toothless comb, the feather of an owl. Wings are beating in the dark above my head. Enormous wings. There is a black river running at my feet, and in its waters blind fish swim and other nameless things that have never known the sun. Now far away a light shines from some fissure in the rock. Shines and is gone. Shines and is gone . . ."

For a long moment the voice was still, almost as if waiting for Erika's hasty writing to catch up. Then it continued. "Those are fearful tendrils creeping between the rocks. They might be serpents or the fingers of a gigantic hand. Slowly, slowly the rocks split; the crack widens, but still there is no light. I know that we are beneath the roots of Yggdrasill, the World Tree. The roots spread like a net — a net cast into the dark sea that laps our feet. We are turning on a wheel of sea and sky, and now suddenly the net is sown with stars, and the stars are terribly close, tangled in the twigs of Yggdrasill. Out on the water there is a light coming closer and closer. Someone is standing in the prow of a boat. In one hand he holds a lamp, in the other a sign I cannot read. There is a message, but it fades as a great bank of fog rolls in. Vassago is anxious to depart. O great Vassago, I give thee license to depart into thy proper place, and be there peace between us evermore. So mote it be."

"There," finished Madame Rose in her normal voice. "You got more than you bargained for. Both more and less, since you still don't know anything, or think you don't. Take your scribbles home and sleep on them — literally, I mean. Under your pillow. Then read them again, and see what you think."

Erika got up slowly, clutching her notes. Her legs trembled slightly, and her joints felt stiff, as if she had been sitting motionless for hours. For some reason the old fortuneteller, who had held her truly spellbound, now seemed less intimidating than she had in her guise of surly charlatan. "Is this what you do, then?" Erika said. "When people come asking about

165

their love lives or their health or whether they're going to get an inheritance. Is this what you do for ten dollars?"

Rose laughed. "You're a good subject, girl, but you're a goose just the same. Of course not. I knew when you stood on the doorstep you were something special."

"Special? What do you mean, special?" Erika asked.

"Never mind what I mean. Come have a cup of tea. Hot and sweet to put you back together again."

In thrall to magic, Erika had almost forgotten the original purpose of her visit, but now she gave a gasp of delight. She was to see more of the house and possibly even meet its other inhabitants. "That would be great," she said, and followed Rose out of the drawing room.

Chapter Nineteen

Erika was dazzled by the flood of colored light from the stained glass skylight in the hall and almost fell over Shadow, who had bounded to his feet when the door to the fortuneteller's parlor opened. He pranced ahead of them, wagging his tail and glancing back at her with shining eyes.

"Looks like he knows you from someplace else," Rose commented. "That's a lot of foolishness, even for him."

"Maybe I've met him in the park," Erika said vaguely.

"Maybe. His young master's very keen on the park."

"Is he?" Erika said, and stopped dead at the kitchen door. "The queen of witches," she whispered, staring across the big room at the woman who stood, smiling slightly, with her back to the fire, a ray of afternoon sun gilding her hair.

"I know you too," Miranda said, stepping forward. "You stood rooted at the edge of the crowd and stared and stared. It was truly gratifying. I also know who it was that took one look and darted away into the dark. We'll have him for desertion, my dear — for quitting his post in the line of fire."

Erika was speechless with a mixture of delight, dismay, and growing comprehension. So it was the sight of his *mother* that had caused Bren to bolt. It was laughable — or was it?

He must have thought that she would step out of the parade and join her son and his new girlfriend for a chat. Would that have been so dreadful? Well, yes, perhaps from Bren's point of view it would have been, for here, surely, was the secret he had been guarding so jealously. It wasn't so much his grandmother's peculiarities that worried Bren as his mother's real and overwhelming witchiness. Here in this charming, domestic room, even more than at the parade, there was not the slightest doubt in Erika's mind that Miranda was the real thing. And Rose, too, she thought with a shiver, remembering the visions that had possessed her only minutes before.

Bren's mother was still smiling at her expectantly, as if waiting for an agreeable but slightly backward child to think of something polite to say. "I'm sorry," Erika blurted. "It's just such a surprise. You must think I'm dumb as a toad."

"What a curious simile," Miranda said. "I mean, it's true that toads are not known for exhilarating discourse, but who would have thought of it?"

"What's all this blather?" Rose filled the kettle and banged it down on the stove. "This girl needs tea, not talk. She's been in the presence of Vassago."

Miranda's eyes widened. "You came to Madame Rose, and you got a full séance? Poor thing. No wonder you're green around the gills."

"No, it was fascinating," Erika protested, but she sank gratefully into a chair at the oak table.

Another thought seemed to strike Bren's mother. "How much did you pay?" she demanded.

"It was nothing," Erika said. "Really. Ten dollars for that experience. I couldn't believe it."

"Mother," Miranda said, stretching out her hand.

To Erika's astonishment, the old woman's face turned red. She fumbled in her apron pocket and brought forth, grudgingly, a crumpled bill and dropped it on the table.

"Take it," Miranda said.

"But I don't . . ." Erika began.

"Take it back," Miranda repeated. "For true witchcraft there can be no charge. It is against the law — the law of the land most places, but also the higher law that we obey."

"Well, how was I to know?" Rose muttered. "I thought she was special when I saw her, but then I thought, all she wants is tall-dark-and-handsome just like the rest of the girls. You say yourself that we can charge for that sort of rubbish."

"If you would be less greedy and collect at the end of the session," Miranda said, "you wouldn't have this problem."

Rose poured out the tea with a venomous glance at her daughter, but said no more. Erika guessed that it was an old argument and pocketed the ten. Now she had time to study the room in which they sat, and here it was easy to remember Bren. A pile of his school books was on the sideboard, and two sneakers, widely separated, on the floor. And here were the things he had described — the comfortable old couch, the cranky, antiquated refrigerator with its wooden doors set into one wall, and the enormous fireplace. She thought of the bleak efficiency of the Apthorp kitchen and envied Bren. Surely it couldn't be so bad to live with two witches in a place like this. Or maybe three. She remembered the black voodoo woman who lived downstairs and wondered if she would be lucky enough to meet her too.

A sudden movement made her jump, and out of nowhere

there was Luna, sitting in the middle of the table, winding her dark tail around her paws and fixing Erika with a blue, unblinking stare.

"Drat that cat," Rose said, but neither woman moved to push her off.

"Meet Luna," Miranda said casually. "Luna is my familiar — my *magistrella*, which means little master. Little mistress, I suppose it should be. Anyway, she's rather a one-woman cat, I'm afraid."

"She's beautiful." Erika stretched out her hand, and the cat, without changing her hieratic pose, leaned forward to sniff the proffered fingers. Slowly the girl who knew nothing about cats reached up and stroked a spot behind one silky ear, and Luna closed her eyes and rubbed her head against the caressing hand.

"Will you look at that," Rose breathed.

"Well, she's *supposed* to be a one-woman cat," Miranda said lightly but with just a trace of jealousy in her voice.

"I'm beginning to think I want a cat," Erika said. "If Luna ever has kittens, I'd love to have one of hers."

"Ha. She wants the spawn of a witch's cat," Rose chuckled. "Maybe she wants to *be* a witch, Miranda. What do you think? We could do a grand job of teaching her."

"I doubt she does," Miranda said. "She's Bren's girlfriend, don't forget."

"Absolutely not," Erika said, with more vehemence than she had intended. "But thank you very much just the same. As for being Bren's girlfriend, I'm really not anymore. We had an awful row after he dumped me at the parade. He called me up, and I pretty much told him to get lost and stay lost. He was drunk, I think. At least he said he was." Why am I saying all this? she wondered. I hardly know these people.

Miranda cast an amused glance at the brown bottle on the mantel. "Yes, drowning his sorrows in his father's Scotch. I suspected as much when I saw what a lot was gone. It had to be either Bren or our mad opera singer in the attic. Witches don't drink, as a rule. Neither does Bren in any interesting way, and that should tell you right there how upset he was."

"I suppose that's true," Erika said dubiously, "but there are things you shouldn't say, because they can never be unsaid."

"Nonsense. People say and unsay things all the time — a lot worse things than you or Bren would even be able to think of." Miranda reached for the kettle and added to Erika's tea. "Still, something must be done to straighten things out. We'll put our minds to it and come up with something good, never fear."

"Ask Louise," Rose suggested. "She knows love charms backward and forward, strange as that might seem."

"But look," Erika said hastily, before Miranda could make another contribution. "This is all unnecessary. Please don't think I'm being ungrateful, but I see now what went wrong, and if it's going to get fixed, I'm afraid I'm the one who has to fix it. You see I do understand why Bren didn't want me to know about the two of you. It's all awfully silly, but I understand. I'll have to think about it and figure it out myself."

"Bren is deplorably conventional," his mother remarked.

"Maybe what I should do," Erika went on, "is tell him I've been here and I love it, so what's all the fuss about?"

"Boring and inadequate," Miranda said.

"But it's *my* love life," Erika protested, laughing, and then

171

realized that it wasn't entirely anymore, because once you involved a witch in something, you were really asking for interference. She knew little about witches, but already she sensed that for them interference was a way of life.

"The attraction is a little weak," Miranda continued. "He's not quite willing to die for you. But that's easy to fix."

"I'm not sure I want him willing to die for me," Erika said, "and it really shouldn't be necessary."

Miranda gave her a stern glance. "Of course not, but the desire should be there. Just let me think." She got up with a swift, feline movement and walked over to the window that gave onto the back yard. For a moment she stared out, then, with a low exclamation, jerked up the sash, and the stillness of the room was filled with a terrified squawking noise and a hoarse voice cursing vigorously in a strange tongue.

"Louise!" Miranda shouted from the window. "Louise, stop that at once, or we'll have the police here."

The curses ceased abruptly, although the squawking continued at a somewhat lower level, as if terror were giving way to mere indignation.

"Black bastard don't want to be caught," came an aggrieved voice, "and I got a meeting to go to."

"Use a little chicken feed," suggested Miranda, "but first, do me a huge favor and come up here, Louise. I need advice." Her voice, Erika noticed, had turned from command to cajolery. There was a grumbling sound, followed by the banging of what was presumably the back door to the basement apartment. Erika wriggled happily in her seat, knowing she was about to meet a third and even more exotic witch.

Miranda shut the window. "I'm glad Bob wasn't here," she

observed. "After I told him we never noticed the chickens."

"You actually keep chickens in your back yard?" Erika asked. This was a detail Bren had neglected to mention.

"Not I," Miranda said with a sniff. "Louise keeps them for some distressing ceremony of her own. She's a black witch, you know. I mean figuratively as well as literally. But we're very fond of her."

Heavy steps could be heard below, and then Louise herself appeared in the kitchen doorway, disheveled and angry but still undeniably regal. "Better be important, babe," she said. "I got only one hour to catch that cock from hell and carry him up to Harlem." She seemed to notice Erika for the first time. "Since when we talk business in front of strangers? You gone off your head, Miranda?"

"This is Erika," Miranda said. "Erika is Bren's girlfriend, and she needs a little help."

"I don't," Erika said, but was ignored.

Louise appeared to forget the urgency of her chicken chase in the wonder of this information. She chuckled richly and advanced into the room. "Bren have a girlfriend now? Will wonders never cease." Joining the group at the kitchen table, she sat down with her chin in her hand and studied Erika with her small, bright eyes. "Skinny," she concluded after a moment, "but bright. Not real seductive, maybe, but there's ways to fix that." Louise laughed again. "There's ways to make him fancy a blind pig, come to that. Pretty girl like you should be no problem."

"But I don't really want to be helped," Erika said. "I know that sounds rude; I just feel that some things you have to do for yourself, and making up with your boyfriend is one of them." She was beginning to feel quite outnumbered by the three witches scheming in her behalf but without her consent.

"Just a little philter," Miranda said.

Erika shook her head. "Not even a little one."

The witches exchanged glances, and Erika had the distinct feeling that they were agreeing to carry on without her cooperation. Miranda made a graceful little gesture of defeat. "Then we'll just have to wish you the best of luck," she said. "Don't forget that we're always here, ready and willing to help if conventional methods bog down, as they so often do."

"Oh, I won't," Erika promised. "And I'm really grateful. Please believe me. It's been fabulous meeting the three of you, and Vassago, of course," she added with a special smile for Rose.

"Angels defend us," the old woman muttered. "She sounds as if she'd met one of the dark lords at a tea party."

"Look that way to me, too," Louise said, with a glance around the cozy table littered with cups and saucers.

Miranda laughed. "Rose gave her the full treatment," she explained, "and then brought her in for a little refreshment."

Erika peeked at her watch and saw to her consternation that it was four o'clock. Bren might be here in less than ten minutes. She pushed back her chair.

"Oh, stay just a little longer, Erika," Miranda begged. "I wanted so much to ask you about the play."

In spite of her panic, Erika was stopped in her tracks. "The play?" she asked. "You mean *Macbeth?* What about it?"

"I saw some of the technical rehearsal," Miranda said, "and it struck me very forcibly that there was a set of problems worthy of my powers. I met your director, too. Such a nice young man. It would be a real pleasure to give him a hand. I know I could do wonders with the lighting and special effects if I just had a little more information."

Erika was appalled and felt sure that Bren would be even more so. It also struck her as unlikely that Mr. Behrens would welcome the assistance of the supernatural. She forced herself to remain calm. "I'm afraid this is another problem that's better left to the people involved," she said, "especially since it's really the last minute. Maybe if you had been in on it from the beginning, but even then, I really don't think . . ." She became aware that she had lost her audience. Louise was leaning across the table, staring at Miranda with gleaming eyes.

"Now that be a truly fine idea," she declared. "Miranda, babe, you finally come up with something worth doing. Meeting and cockerel be damned. I can stand to spend some time on this."

Miranda's eyes sparkled at the compliment, and Erika saw that the other two really held the black woman in awe. "Do you really like it, Lou? Will you help?" Miranda cried. "It's not any easy thing, and I'm still racking my brains about it."

"Kinetic power you gonna need, Miranda," Louise said. "Piles and piles of kinetic power. You think you can pull it off?"

"Never by myself," Miranda said. "Not for a minute. I'm good, but I'm not that good. Is there a balcony in your theater?" She turned suddenly to Erika, who was startled into answering.

"Yes, but we almost never use it."

"You'll get us three seats in the front of the balcony," Miranda said.

"But I can't," Erika protested. "They won't let you go up, not if it's really closed, and anyway, I don't think . . ."

"You don't need to think, my dear," said Rose, "nor to worry about any little rules and regulations. You just dance and say your lines, and if Miranda wants seats in the balcony for herself and a whole platoon of Marines, she'll get them, I promise you. It's one of the things she's good at."

"All right!" Erika cried. She was now frantic to be gone. "All right. I don't see how I can stop you, and I absolutely have to run. I just realized that I'm horribly late. Thank you all so much for everything!" She backed to the door, carrying with her the image of the three women who seemed so determined to take her life in charge, gathered around the table with the beautiful, mysterious cat seated like a royal effigy in their midst. The black dog lay with his nose pressed against the crack in the front door. Waiting for his master, she thought, then jerked open the door and collided with Bren, who was standing on the stoop looking through the mail.

Bren staggered back, dropping the mail and his school books into the clump of rhododendron bushes. "Erika!" he shouted. "What are you doing here?"

"Nothing to do with you," Erika said quickly, clutching the railing to regain her balance. "I came to see your grandmother. She advertises, you know — little cards in coffee shops."

"In a pig's eye. You were snooping."

"Why would I want to do that?" Erika asked. "I came to have my fortune told. I'm really into the supernatural, you know. Or didn't you? I forget."

"You are not," Bren growled. "You're into snooping, and you're into driving me crazy. As if I didn't have enough problems."

"You dropped everything in the bushes," Erika observed. She was not really trying to be infuriating. She was trying to think what she could do or say to improve this hideous encounter. The remark, however, had not been well chosen.

"You have a gift for this kind of thing," Bren said. "You were born to be maddening. What do I care if I dropped an entire library in the bushes? What I want to know is what you were doing in my house."

"I told you," Erika said. "I came to see your grandmother. I was all mixed up, and I wanted someone to look into a crystal ball and tell me everything was going to be all right. That's the truth, Bren."

"But not the whole truth," he said. He was really looking at her now and getting pains in his chest as he always did when he looked at Erika. To his surprise, she reached out her hand and pulled him down onto the top step of the stoop.

"No, of course not," she said. "The truth is I couldn't stop thinking about you, and when I found out about your grandmother, I felt I had to come and see if I could figure out the rest — you know, why you were always disappearing at odd moments and what there was about your house that I wasn't supposed to know. I met your mother too, and Louise and Luna."

Bren groaned and put his head in his hands. "Well, now you know, anyway," he said in a muffled voice.

Erika stroked the back of his neck. "Now I know, and I think it's all amazing and wonderful," she said. "How could you think I wouldn't, Bren? Did you think I was some kind of nitwit who wanted everything to be like a TV cereal commercial?"

Bren lifted his head and smiled uncertainly. "Never," he

177

said. "Not for a minute, but, you know, there's normal, and then there's different enough to be interesting, and then there's my place. The gap between the last two, I've always thought, is unreasonably large."

"We don't really know each other very well," Erika said. "How could we? And what happens is we keep making these ludicrous mistakes and then getting angry and upset."

Bren stared at her. "There should be a way around that," he said, "for two people who aren't terminally stupid."

"Like seeing more of each other?" Erika suggested. "Like talking to each other and telling the truth, at least part of the time, and taking walks and doing things together and what-not?"

"And lots and lots of what-not," Bren said, putting his hands behind her head and closing the small gap that remained between them.

Through the massive front door there came an anguished yelp and a thump as Shadow, his patience tried beyond endurance, threw himself against the barrier that separated him from his friends. Erika and Bren sprang apart, suddenly aware of where they were — of the public nature of a front stoop in Manhattan and of the existence of other creatures in the universe.

"We could begin by taking Shadow to the park," Bren said, "and carry on from there."

"And on and on," said Erika, scrambling joyfully to her feet. "And on and on and on!"

Chapter Twenty

"Once more unto the breach, dear friends," cried Edward Behrens, borrowing shamelessly from a different play.

"And close the wall up with our Perkins dead," an unidentified voice suggested from the back of the room.

The entire cast and crew of *Macbeth* were assembled in the tiny greenroom of the Perkins Theater to hear the theatrical version of the pep talk before the big game.

"It will go wonderfully well, you know," their director continued, and they gazed at him in mute, terrified adoration. "You have all heard about bad dress rehearsals being followed by smashing first night performances, and I want to assure you that this is absolutely true. I have seen it hundreds of times," said Mr. Behrens, who had personal experience of perhaps ten productions. His eyes roved over his small and, at this moment, much-loved band of students, and he felt a wave of genuine confidence and admiration. "Polly, just one little tuft more on the left side of that ravishing beard, my dear. Macduff, your ears are still shockingly white. Don't worry. You've plenty of time to put it right, and really, you all look splendid. Now go out there and sock it to them!"

"Is it really true about bad dress rehearsals?" Bren asked Eli as they climbed the stairs to the light booth.

"Could be, but don't count on it," Eli said. "If you ask me, it's one of those things like walking under a ladder. If somebody drops a bucket of paint on your head, the superstition is confirmed. If not, you forget about it. Same thing with rehearsals. If all goes well tonight, everyone will remember the old saw. If it bombs, it won't count. Why? Are you scared?"

"No. Should I be?" Bren asked, hoping that Eli could not detect the thundering of his heart against his ribs.

Eli shrugged and ducked into the light booth. "I don't see why," he said. "After all, we're the wonder boys of Perkins Theater. You're just kind of a funny color."

"Haven't been getting my daily sunshine," Bren said, following Eli into their familiar little den. He was, in fact, suffering from stage fright despite the vast improvement in the lighting since the first technical. The reconciliation with Erika had, he felt, transformed him utterly from a wretched, miserable incompetent into someone strong, brave, and confident in the exercise of his craft. The disasters that had continued to plague the cast and stage crew had left him largely untouched, but now it was opening night, and he was petrified.

"All systems go," said Eli, after a swift check of cue sheets and switches. "And now we wait."

Bren sat down at the switchboard and looked out over the empty balcony to the rapidly filling main floor of the theater. There, neither too far up nor too far back, he saw his father's broad shoulders and fashionably tousled hair. And there, making stately progress toward the front row, was Madame Lavatky in a costume that would have done credit to an opening at La Scala.

A buzzer sounded in the light booth, and Bren began the slow fade of the house lights. Gradually the babble of the audience died away and was replaced by the expectant hush that is the special delight of all who love the theater. Bren's eyes, straining to catch the parting of the curtains, his cue to bring up the lights for the opening scene, missed the arrival of three women who, in the moment of darkness before the play, slipped into seats in the front row of the balcony.

Now the stillness was broken by a rumble of thunder, and lightning flashed in the shadows far upstage. A white spotlight stabbed down onto the apron, and into its dazzling circle leapt Erika. Bren caught his breath, for she seemed to materialize out of nowhere at the same instant as the light. It was the effect they had striven for and never quite achieved.

> "When shall we three meet again
> In thunder, lightning, or in rain?"

Rushing in from the wings, the other witches joined her, and Bren brought up two more of the big lico lights, one blue, one green. The three girls were wonderfully hideous as they huddled together and plotted their fateful meeting with Macbeth. Chortling and hugging each other in an obscene parody of sisterhood, they chanted hoarsely,

> "Fair is foul and foul is fair,
> Hover through the fog and filthy air."

They circled once more in the light and fled into blackness at the sides of the stage as thunder rolled and the light was quenched.

In the next instant the main stage was washed with the harsh light of a stormy afternoon, and Jeremy's ghastly tree was silhouetted against an ominous sky. Bren sat back with a sigh, knowing he could relax while the king and his attendants described the distant battle and the heroic deeds of Macbeth. The second witch scene was at least five minutes away.

That scene went well too, technically and in every other way. Even as he met the demands of a gathering storm and a slowly darkening stage, Bren found time to be amazed at the performance of the three witches. Erika moved as if she were a bundle of jointless bones animated by some evil puppeteer. She capered around the tree and rummaged for revolting treasures in her tattered shopping bag. ("Here I have a pilot's thumb, Wracked as homeward he did come.") Macbeth and Banquo, frail, noble figures from the world of light, listened to the prophecy that would make Macbeth both king and murderer. Then came an even more frenzied dance, then blackout and a perfect vanishment.

"Oh glory, glory, glory," whispered Eli in the back of the light booth. "We'll never do that again."

"Sure we will," Bren whispered back, as he moved the dials that restored the stage to its previous state of ordinary gloom.

The play proceeded, not without minor mishaps, but on the whole remarkably well. Shifting from one foot to the other and trying not to pace up and down behind the last row of seats, Edward Behrens wondered what he had done to deserve this seeming triumph. It's not that I haven't done plenty, he reflected, remembering hours of effort and excruciating patience, but this — this is a blooming miracle.

The king had been killed by Macbeth, and soon his body would be found. Behrens relaxed slightly and smiled as he watched the brief comic scene (the only one the grim play affords) in which the porter is awakened by the late arrival of Macduff. Now came the horrific discovery scene and the lighting sequence Bren had bungled so thoroughly in the Saturday rehearsal. It should go well again, as it had the last two nights. Behrens spared a moment to be grateful to Eli for talking him out of replacing Bren.

In the light booth Bren leaned forward, listening for the cue to begin the subtle changes that would precede the discovery of the murdered king. The moment came, and his hands moved on the switchboard. The cues unfolded as he had planned them. All around him in the high, shadowy corners of the theater where he had labored so long, the lights faded and bloomed.

Onstage Macbeth's grim castle slowly emerged against a starless sky. Light from the porter's lamp spilled across ancient stones and touched the tired faces of the men gathered in the courtyard. It had been a night of evil omens, but now it was time to wake the king. Reluctantly Macduff took up the lamp and went to the door of Duncan's chamber. For a moment the door yawned black in the castle wall. Then light flared within, and Macduff staggered forth with his terrible cry, "Oh horror, horror, horror! Tongue nor heart cannot conceive nor name thee!" The sky flushed with the sullen red of dawn, and the very air seemed suddenly suffused with blood.

Bren watched the shifting, mingling beams from his big spotlights with intense satisfaction. He could hardly believe that only a few weeks ago this mystery had been closed to him, and now this power of transformation was in his hands. I have my own witchcraft now, he thought with a wry smile, but mine is real. I've got calluses and a couple of burns to prove it.

At intermission, while Eli faded the last scene, Bren was already on his way backstage to look for Erika. He therefore failed for a second time to notice the occupants of the balcony.

Miranda, flanked by her sister witches, was enjoying herself, but even she had opening-night nerves. She had never tried anything on this scale before or anything that involved so much sheer mental power acting over so great a distance. "It a lot like changing the weather," Louise had said. "And you a real champion at that, babe. Besides, we build that old pyramid of power together, don't you forget that." Miranda still felt that it was her show and she might just screw it up. This was a poor attitude for a witch in need of total concentration. So she had bided her time, soaking up the atmosphere of the terrifying play, letting its dark mysteries charge her mind. Now, as the lights dimmed for the second half, she felt ready for the coming trial. Her eyes glowed like sapphires in the gloom, and her body tingled with energy. "What we waitin' for?" Louise grumbled in a low voice. "I want to watch Shakespeare, I can rent him from the VCR place, put my feet up and have a beer."

"Just a little longer," Miranda whispered back. "I know what I'm waiting for, Lou, and it will be worth the wait, I promise you."

Later Miranda was to swear with perfect truth that she

had done nothing to influence the first two thirds of opening night at the Perkins School. "Each important event has its own aura," she explained, "and the aura for this performance was especially good. That's the long and the short of it, my dears."

And perhaps it was. Certainly there is a tide which, on certain unforgettable occasions, will sweep a production forward from one fine moment to the next. Each high point builds upon the one before, and astonishment gives way to confidence in the inevitability of victory. So it was that night with *Macbeth*.

In the back of the house Edward Behrens congratulated himself on the emotional hardihood that had enabled him to put up with Brian Rushmore. The temperamental boy actor had disappeared, and in his place a tormented Scottish king struggled in the toils of pride and fear. The banquet scene began. Macbeth's terror was real, and so, to Behrens's relief, was Banquo's ghost. It was possible to believe in the ghastly apparition that rose so convincingly from the hollowed-out end of Jeremy's banquet table. It was even possible to believe that Macbeth saw it and no one else did. The tension grew, and the guests dispersed, suspicious and disturbed. Alone with his terrible consort Macbeth cried out, "It will have blood, they say: blood will have blood."

During the next scene, quiet and threatening, in which Lennox and another lord voiced their suspicions of Macbeth, the director crossed his fingers and prayed for witches and apparitions to match the wonders that had gone before. And in the small booth above his head, Eli slid from his seat, and Bren sat down at the board with a pounding heart. He was afraid again, and in a rather different way from his earlier attack of stage fright. It was a sensation that was difficult to account for. Downstage the two men parted, and the lights went out.

From the wings, Erika listened to the rumble of the cauldron being rolled into place and looked out into the black cavern of the theater. Suddenly her eyes widened. Like Banquo's ghost, it was a thing not everyone could see, and this was just as well, for at the balcony rail stood three figures outlined in flickering blue fire. To Erika's terrified eyes, they seemed abnormally tall. Even the grandmother appeared to have grown, and her white hair crackled in the uncanny light. With joined hands they stood and stared down onto the darkened stage. Erika felt Miranda's eyes boring into the corner where she crouched and covered her face with her hands. Then there was a hiss behind her, and a strong push in the middle of her back sent her stumbling out onto the stage seconds before the end of the blackout.

Thunder cracked, and there was a sound of rising wind. A streak of lightning showed for a moment the smoking cauldron and the three witches crouched around it. Darkness was followed by light of such an extraordinarily evil quality that a low murmur of fear went through the audience.

> *First Witch:* Thrice the brinded cat hath mew'd.
> *Second Witch:* Thrice, and once the hedge-pig whin'd.
> *Third Witch:* Harper cries: 'Tis time, 'tis time.
> *First Witch:* Round about the cauldron go;
> In the poison'd entrails throw.
> Toad, that under cold stone
> Days and nights hast thirty-one
> Swelter'd venom sleeping got,

Boil thou first i' the charmed pot.
All: Double, double toil and trouble;
Fire burn and cauldron bubble.

The rising steam turned red as Bren's trembling hand brought up the special spot, but the witches' faces seemed lit from within by the fires of hell. Gray rags became gray flaps of skin, pendulous and horrible, hanging from the swaying bodies of the dancers. Frightful things went into the pot — scales and eyes, livers and lips — and now, slowly, a thick, pervasive stench began to invade the theater as if vapors from that unholy brew were drifting forth on the rising wind.

The incantation ended, but the dance went on. The first witch seemed to levitate and fly through the darkening air. The others followed with a shriek, faster and faster, until at another thunder clap they dropped to all fours, staring into the distance.

"By the pricking of my thumbs,
Something wicked this way comes,"

muttered the second witch, and Macbeth was there, blustering and desperate, to demand his future of the forces of darkness.

In the light booth, Eli moved as if in a trance, slipping the first slide into the projector. "First apparition, an armed head," he mumbled, and was relieved to see the head appear on the scrim at the back of the stage. "Now for the bloody child," he said. But the bloody child had been improved. The scrim wavered, and the blood ran. Someone in the audience gave a low whimper, and Brian's voice shook as he demanded a

187

third apparition, a child crowned, with a tree in its hand. Child and tree appeared, and the tree was green as all the fields of spring, its branches stirred by a freshening breeze.

Still Macbeth is not satisfied. He has been warned to beware Macduff but also that he cannot be brought down by any man of woman born, nor defeated until Birnam Wood shall come to Dunsinane. But what of his heirs and of the prophecy that Banquo's children will be kings?

"Seek to know no more!" the witches cry, but Macbeth is adamant. No one can doubt his courage or his foolhardiness as he stands his ground in the raging gale.

Tonight there is no jerkiness or overlap of slides to mar the procession of the nine kings across the scrim. The kings are there — eight in the likeness of Banquo, followed by Banquo himself, carrying a mirror in which is seen, hugely magnified, an endless progression of identical crowned figures moving away into some unimaginably remote place and time, all kings of Scotland, while Macbeth lies in an unremembered grave.

Bent now upon cheering their ravaged guest, the witches dance again with a perverted jollity. They prod each other's wobbling flesh and scream with mirth, while all about them the tempest roars, and the air crackles with blue light. Then suddenly they are gone, and in the throbbing darkness of the theater, the voice of Macbeth cries out:

> "Where are they? Gone? Let this pernicious hour
> Stand aye accursed in the calendar!
> Come in, without there!"

For a moment nothing happened. "Bring up the lights!" Eli hissed.

"I can't," Bren whispered. "It's been taken out of my hands." But somehow he managed to start the next cue, and the stage was flooded with ordinary light for the return of Lennox.

In the balcony Miranda sank back in her seat. "Enough, do you think?" she murmured.

"Let's take a breather and then do a number on that crazy walking woodland," said Louise, mopping her brow with an enormous purple handkerchief.

And so it was that the luckless extras who carried their green branches onto the battlefield were scarcely seen. True, it was possible to make out the occasional arm and leg, for the movement of the forest was, after all, only a strategy. But the "boughs" specified by Shakespeare had grown into sizable trees. Their advance upon the beleaguered forces of Macbeth had the quality of a nightmare dreamed by the mad king himself — he who now grew "aweary of the sun" and yet stood fast, shouting to his men,

> "Ring the alarum bell! Blow wind, come wrack,
> At least we'll die with harness on our back."

The forest marched, and once again the parents and friends of Shakespeare at the Perkins School shifted uneasily in their seats. In the back of the house stood a much-shaken Edward Behrens. "There's still the fight," he said under his breath, "and if Brian carries this off, he gets a gold medal and the right to be obnoxious for the rest of his life."

Chapter Twenty-One

Unable for once to think of a quotation, Mr. Behrens punched his victorious Macbeth on the shoulder as the actors came backstage after their curtain call. "I am speechless with admiration, Brian," he said. "Truly speechless, believe it or not."

"Thanks, old man. It was really no problem," Brian said with a gracious inclination of his head.

"Oh, Bear!" cried Lady Macbeth. "Wasn't it all too wonderful and weird?" She threw her arms around him with something between a laugh and a sob and deposited a large smear of makeup on his white shirt.

He patted her head, wondering why it sometimes seemed that only the brainless could act, and looked around for Erika. "It was both," he said, "and you were extra marvelous. So were you all," he added for the benefit of anyone else within hearing.

When he was able to disentangle himself from the rest of the cast, he found the first witch, alone in the wings and staring out at the empty stage. Her expression was at once ecstatic and terrified. "Tell me what you did," said Behrens, without compliments or preamble.

"I didn't do anything," Erika said. "It just happened, Bear, and it scared me out of my wits."

He looked at her in silence for a moment, then reached out and gave her a gentle shake. "Things like that don't just happen," he said. "In fact, they don't happen at all, but never mind for now. Pull yourself together, girl. We've laid on a party after the show, and you must be there looking like a normal witch instead of one who just escaped from the funny farm."

"Oh, God, I suppose I must," Erika said, and produced a wan smile.

At the announcement following the play of "a small reception for family and friends of the company," several members of the audience were seen to leave the theater in haste with the comment that what they needed was a good stiff drink. They were unaware that Perkins, a private school, would be attentive to the needs of its parents. There were two punch bowls, one for guests and one for students; and since Jeremy had taken care of the latter with a large bottle of vodka, there was little to choose between them.

Bren found Erika backstage, where cast and crew were scurrying to get into street clothes for the party. She had taken off the worst of her makeup and put on a black leotard and skirt. Her efforts to comb the stiff spikes of pink hair had met with little success. It looked, if anything, more tortured than before, and the lingering smudges of black greasepaint around her eyes gave her a haunted look.

"You were phenomenal," Bren said, giving her a hug. "Awesome, marvelous, incredible, out of this world."

Erika clung to him for a moment and then stepped back. "Incredible and out of this world?" she said. "I think I have to agree with you. It was scary, Bren. I felt almost . . . I don't know what to say. Almost possessed. It wasn't a nice feeling, however wonderful the results."

Bren frowned. "I know what you mean. We felt it too, and things happened with the lights that never happened before — good things like making you vanish so perfectly, but some others we never even thought of, that we wouldn't even know how to do. I don't know what to think."

"It was almost," Erika said carefully, "as if someone or something was working on the play in a supernatural way. I know this sounds far-fetched. I don't suppose it's even the kind of thing she could do, but, well, you know what I'm thinking."

Bren stared at her. "That's crazy," he said. "I'm sure she couldn't do anything like that. Certainly not without being here, and she couldn't be here without my knowing it."

Erika found that her reluctance to tell him what she had seen had evaporated. After all, they were in this together now and had made a pledge of frankness on the still difficult subject of Bren's witchy relatives. "I saw her, Bren," she confessed. "I saw all three of them. They were standing in the front of the balcony, and there was a sort of blue fire playing around them. It was just before the last big witch scene."

"Now she's gone too far," said Bren, not for the first time in his life. "This has got to stop."

"Do you think they'll come to the party?" Erika asked.

"Can you think of anything that would be likely to stop them?" Bren countered with a cynical smile. "Half the fun would be hearing what people had to say about the special effects."

Erika peeked through the curtain in back of the stage. "I suppose we'd better put in an appearance," she said dubiously. "It's all set up, and people have started to arrive."

Onstage the towers and battlements had been pushed back, although they still loomed in the corners. The banquet table had been set up again, its flagons and papier-mâché suckling pig replaced with plastic glasses and the two punch bowls. A number of parents had already gathered at one end of the table, and some of the company were dipping enthusiastically into Jeremy's concoction at the other when Bren and Erika joined them. Miranda and her two colleagues were nowhere to be seen.

Inevitably, as the terrors of the play faded, spectators and cast began to look for an explanation of what they had seen. What could be more obvious than to hold the light crew responsible? Lighting was perceived to be in the realm of science, and everyone knew that science moved in mysterious ways. Aesthetic questions were also being raised, and not everyone was pleased. A tall man with something of Brian's self-satisfied expression, who turned out to be the theater's founder and patron, cornered Bren. "You technical people do incredible things," he said. "Congratulations and all that, but one wonders if you don't sometimes lose your sense of proportion."

"Proportion?" Bren said vaguely, burying his nose in his punch. "Oh yes, sometimes. Maybe."

"After all," the great actor continued, "the play's the thing, my boy, don't you know? There were times tonight when the special effects were quite overwhelming. And other times when they weren't. It was uneven, if you see what I mean."

"I do," Bren said. "I think you're one hundred percent right. Excuse me." He had caught sight of his mother, flanked by Louise and Rose, at the far side of the stage. Suspicion, turning rapidly into certainty, flooded his mind as he stared at the radiant figure of his parent.

Miranda wore a dress of cornflower-blue silk, its high neck and simple lines a perfect setting for a remarkable necklace of rough-cut amethysts. Not every woman would have added the curiously knotted gold cord around her waist, but Miranda had never had any trouble carrying off the accessories that were the tools of her trade. Just as a window washer goes about draped in pails and coils of rope, so did Miranda adorn herself for an evening of mixed business and pleasure. Bren had no need of X-ray eyes to know that under the shimmering blue silk of his mother's skirt was a red garter embroidered with cabalistic signs, and that on the slender hand now delving into an enormous pocketbook was an intricate gold ring with a high crown and a little knob like the catch to a box.

Intent on composing a suitably scathing speech, Bren failed to see Madame Lavatky until he was enveloped in her arms. She smelled strongly of gardenias mingled with the whiff of an exotic but all too familiar beverage. "Darlink Bren! It is so beautiful I am crying all the time," Madame exclaimed. She released him with one hand so that she could dab at the corner of a purple-shadowed eye.

"Thanks, Madame Lavatky. I'm glad you could come. What a nice surprise," Bren said, tugging at his imprisoned arm.

"Never, never in my long life of art do I see such things," the opera singer continued. "Not at the Met, not at La Scala, not at Bayreuth — never such atmosphere, such evoking of the soul. It is unbelievable."

"That's true," Bren said. "I have to admit I was just a bit surprised myself. Excuse me a minute. I see my mother over there."

"Yes, yes. Run to your mother. She is crazy with joy and pride."

"But not in me," Bren muttered, as he pulled away from Madame Lavatky and began pushing through the crowd.

"Hi, Mom," he said, drawing up in front of the guilty trio. "Hi, Gram. Hi, Louise. It's great you all managed to get here. I didn't see you come in."

"Congratulations, darling." Miranda leaned forward and brushed his cheek with her lips. "We were in the balcony. Such a wonderful view of all those marvelous lighting effects."

"Nobody was supposed to go onto the balcony," Bren said. "I've got cables running all over the place. Who let you go up?"

"A very nice young man," his mother said, and Bren groaned. There probably wasn't an usher alive who could have stopped Miranda from sitting where she chose to sit, much less the wimp he now remembered had been posted at the balcony stairs.

"I see it all," Bren said. "At least, I hardly see it all. I see where it was done, but as to how and, for God's sake, *why*, I don't suppose I'll ever know."

"Here comes the first witch," Miranda commented brightly. "Such a talented girl, Bren. Do you know her?"

"Yes, I know her, and you know I know her," Bren said, as Erika came to stand beside him. "I don't think any introductions are called for, so stop playing games with me, Mom, and tell me what you were doing up in the balcony."

"Hey, Erika, you a fine witch, girl," said Louise. "Who would have thought it? You miss your calling for sure."

Erika looked uneasily from one to the other, wondering how far the conversation had progressed. "Thanks, Louise," she said. "But it's just dancing, you know, and great makeup and, of course, lights and . . . and things."

Rose chuckled. " 'And things,' she says. Things there were, no doubt about it, but only part of the time. You were a lovely witch, my dear, all things aside, and that makeup was a wonder. Hard to believe three young girls could get to looking a hundred years old with just a little goo smeared on their faces."

Erika glanced at Bren, who was still glaring at his mother, and wondered if they should be left alone together. "It isn't exactly a little goo," she said. "It's quite an amazing lot, and pieces of hair and soft plastic, and all sorts of stuff. Come on down to the makeup room, and I'll show you."

Louise, who had wandered off and was poking at the painted canvas skin of one of the towers, followed Erika and Rose backstage, leaving Bren and Miranda together.

"You didn't really mind, did you?" Miranda asked. "It was such fun, Bren, and such a terrific test of my powers."

"What's the matter with you?" Bren said. "Of course I minded. You threw everything out of whack, and besides, it's going to be a hard act to follow."

"Well, maybe we could come to the other performances,"

Miranda suggested. "I'll ask Louise and Rose, though I don't think they care so much for Shakespeare as I do."

"You've missed the point completely. You always do." Bren was trying to keep his voice down and control the rising tide of exasperation that always accompanied such discussions with his mother. "The point is . . . oh, great. Here comes Behrens. Try to act like a seminormal mom, if you can. He's the director."

"Mr. Behrens and I have already met," Miranda said, holding out her hand. "We had such a fascinating talk after the technical rehearsal."

"At the tech!" Bren cried, then stopped and stared as his mother and his director greeted each other like old friends.

"It's the mysterious lady," Behrens said. "Mother of the lighting genius and major prophetess. I never would have believed it could go so well. You must have done a job of praying because I totally forgot to avoid saying the name of the play."

"I knew you would," Miranda said, "and you see it didn't matter after all. There's always more than one way around a minor curse. I told you it would go well."

"You told me maybe Bren and Erika would start doing their jobs with their usual competence. You didn't tell me they were going to take off into the realm of the supernatural."

"And did they?" Miranda asked with a provocative smile.

"Well, not literally, I suppose," Behrens said uneasily. "I keep telling myself that I didn't see what I thought I saw."

"Always a futile undertaking," said Miranda.

Bren, who had been listening to this conversation with

growing comprehension and alarm, now noticed his father standing by the punch bowl — a solid and comforting sight. "Hey, Dad!" he called, abandoning Behrens to his mother's wiles. "Am I glad you came. What did you think?"

"Great, Bren, really great." Bob put his arm around his son's shoulders for a brief, fatherly squeeze. "Looks as though you've found a career outside of dog walking. No kidding. The lights were wonderful."

"Thanks," Bren said, "but I'm a little sick of them at the moment."

"That'll pass. You've got a real talent there. I see your mother has found a friend. Who the hell is he?"

"Oh, that's just the director, Mr. Behrens," Bren said. "I mean, he's really great, but I don't think they know each other very well. They only met the other night at the rehearsal."

Bob stared at his wife, who was gazing into her companion's eyes and gently stroking the amethyst necklace that glowed on her shimmering blue dress.

"He'd better watch out, whoever he is," Bob said. "He could be in more than one kind of bad, bad trouble."

He's jealous, Bren thought happily, and she's only teasing poor Bear. The party began to seem like more fun. He helped himself to another cup of punch and began to wonder how Erika could stay so long backstage.

"Don't go away," he said. "I want to find somebody you've got to meet."

"I am rooted to the spot," Bob answered, his eyes still fixed on his flirting wife. "How could I tear myself away?"

"Don't be a dingbat," Bren said. "I'll be right back."

Chapter Twenty-Two

Bren's search for Erika, however, was brief and abortive. He had barely turned away from the refreshment table when he saw a sight that froze him in his tracks — a new arrival at the party and, from his point of view, the last straw.

Alia's fiery hair fell to her shoulders, where tiny straps held up a skin-tight sheath of acid green, and she was dripping with witch jewels. Her recovery was obviously complete; her dark eyes glowed, and her tall figure radiated seductive energy. Possibly Miranda, in her newfound preoccupation with the theater, had allowed her malevolent hold on Alia's health to slip. Perhaps Alia was a better witch than anyone had given her credit for. Whatever the cause, her presence promised nothing but a hideously embarrassing scene.

"Dad's really going to love this," Bren muttered, and hurried back to his father. "Don't look now, but a certain sickly redhead is alive and well and coming up fast on our starboard bow," he said.

Bob looked, as people always do when told not to. He turned an interesting shade of plum under his tan. "My God, she looks terrific, doesn't she?" was the first thing he managed to say.

"No," Bren said.

"I think, on the other hand, I'll just fade out, old son, if you don't mind too much. She's going to string me up by my toes for not inviting her tonight."

"Too late," said Bren, as Alia engulfed them both in a wave of Mediterranean charm.

"Ben!" she cried, landing a kiss on his ear when he tried to duck. "It is so long since I see you, and Bobby, too, you wicked man. Why do you not invite me to this wonderful play?"

"Hi, Alia," Bob said. "I thought you were sick."

"Ah, I was so sick you cannot imagine," Alia said enthusiastically. "The pain in every part of my body — my head, my back, my — how do you say, *fegato?*"

"How should I know?" Bob asked crossly.

Alia clutched the lower right side of her abdomen. "Her liver, I think," Bren contributed.

"I'm sorry, but I don't want to hear about it," Bob said, casting a desperate glance in Miranda's direction.

"*Crudele,*" Alia pronounced. "Who would think such a sweet man as your father could be so cruel?" Bren shrugged, and she carried on. "But never mind. As you see, I am perfect now."

"You look great," Bob said. "Really great. I mean it."

"Such a beautiful party," Alia continued, her eyes darting from one group to another. "So many interesting people. Who, I wonder, is that extraordinary blond woman in the blue dress?"

"I don't know," Bren said at the same time that Bob said, "Oh, that's . . . er, Bren's mother."

Alia produced a silvery laugh. "I must meet her and see which one of you is right. Introduce me, Bobby."

"You've got to be kidding," Bob said.

"Well then, I must introduce myself, since Ben cannot take me to meet someone he doesn't know."

"I didn't see who you meant," Bren mumbled, but Alia was already under way, and he could only watch with horrified fascination the impending confrontation. He thought again of going to look for Erika and Louise and Rose. Surely the addition of two more witches to this hellish social brew could not make it any worse. He was prevented from following this impulse by his father, who was clutching his arm. Male solidarity was being called upon, but Bren found it hard to think of any useful contribution he could make. Now he saw that Miranda had stopped abruptly in the middle of some sprightly remark to Behrens and turned to face her rival. Bren suspected that Alia's presence was no surprise to his mother. She had been biding her time.

"I think you are Miranda West," said Alia. "Already I am the friend of your adorable son."

"Oh yes?" Miranda raised her eyebrows in a delicate question mark. "And also, I think, of my adorable husband."

"But of course. We are — how do you say? — colleagues in the office. I am layout artist, I think is the term. You must pardon my English."

"Gladly," said Miranda. "Your English is charming, and 'layout artist' is close, but 'colleague' falls a bit wide of the mark."

Bren was now eavesdropping shamelessly as Alia continued as if she had missed the entire innuendo. "But we have so much in common," she said. "We must become friends."

"Do you think so?" asked Miranda, fixing the other woman with a bright, blue stare.

"Here it comes," Bren whispered to his father. "Now we'll see who's the better witch."

"Witch!" Bob said. "But Alia's not a . . . Oh, my God, Bren!"

Bren gave him a look that was both pitying and incredulous, put his finger to his lips, and nodded toward the two women, who were metaphorically rolling up their sleeves. Behrens stood in the background with his mouth slightly open. No one had bothered to include him in the introductions.

"Of course," Alia was saying. "I did admire your work so much. That blood on the little child and the smell from the cauldron — so effective and hard to do, if just a little coarse."

"Coarse!" cried Miranda. "Of course it was coarse. What did you want? Sweet lavender, rosemary, and thyme?"

"Naturally not," Alia said in a soothing voice. "I do not criticize. It was truly a marvel. The marching of the trees, too, and the quality of light. Not easy at all. Of course, you had help, but it was most impressive for an amateur."

"Amateur!" Miranda said furiously, and Bren began to fear that she was losing at least the verbal part of the battle. Any more telling response was cut off by Edward Behrens, who had now revived sufficiently to be both indignant and curious.

"I don't like to interfere," he said, "in what is clearly a private dispute. On the other hand . . ."

"You're quite right," Miranda said quickly. "We're being rude. So boring to listen to people talk shop."

"Not at all. I found it riveting, but I do think you owe me an explanation, like just what the hell did you do to my play?"

Miranda put her hand on his arm. "Nothing really," she said. "Just a little thought transference — a little psychic boost here and there. Please don't be upset."

"Come to me next time," Alia suggested. "I will make real bats fly out of your witch's cauldron."

"Bats! Who wants bats? All I asked for was a nice, smooth production — not too many missed cues, not too many blown lines — and what did I get? Blood. Smells. People flying. Now you offer me bats, and who are you, by the way?"

"I am one who practices the great art of Wicca," said Alia grandly. "She, too, could be said to dabble in these things."

"I'll give you dabble. Dabble indeed, you cheap, ignorant, Neapolitan fake!" Miranda cried, whirling on Alia.

Behrens stepped deftly between the two witches, who seemed about to carry their quarrel into the realm of hair pulling or possibly something worse. "You two beauties can fight it out later," he said firmly. "I just want to be quite clear about one thing. You're trying to tell me that one of you bewitched my production of *Macbeth* and the other one thinks she could have done it better. Is that right?"

"That's right," Alia said.

"Something like that," said Miranda.

"I don't believe it."

Miranda laughed. "Well, you can't have it both ways, dear Bear. Either you saw what you thought you saw, or you didn't. Make up your mind."

"I didn't," Behrens said. "I am a scientist first and a stage director second. I am suffering from nervous exhaustion at the moment, but that will pass with the help of a few more drinks. It's been a pleasure meeting both of you, but I am going to leave you now to your curious grievances. Good night."

Miranda watched, smiling a little ruefully, as the director made a dignified but hasty retreat to the punch bowl. "Such a nice man," she said, "and he wouldn't have had a clue if a certain mean and jealous person hadn't come along to disillusion him."

"The day will never come that I will be jealous of you," Alia snapped. "You are small tomatoes."

"Potatoes," Miranda said, "but don't worry, my dear. Your English will improve, if you can keep your health."

Alia's eyes bulged. "Ah, so it was you! Fiend of the devil, beware! You will not sleep another night without pain. Your teeth will fall out. Your hair will be gray."

"Hey, Bren," Bob said. "Do you think I am really witch-prone? I mean, do you think I have to have a witch?"

Bren nodded emphatically. "You're doomed," he said. "It's obviously a fatal attraction. All you can do is decide which witch. There must be a better way to say that."

"I know which," Bob declared in a loud voice, "and I'm going to get her out of here before one of them witches the other into extinction."

"Be careful," Bren cried, as his father stepped resolutely between Alia and Miranda.

Miranda greeted his sudden appearance with relief. "Oh, Bob," she said, "I've been dying to talk to you. How did you like the play? Didn't Bren do a wonderful job with the lights?"

Alia, who now found herself looking at Bob's back, made a little circling maneuver, which he, as if he had eyes in the back of his head, immediately countered, so that she remained shut out of the conversation. She stepped back a pace and stood staring at her former lover and his wife. Her face had turned white, and her hands were clenched at her sides.

"The play was terrific," Bob said, "and so were you — meddling as usual, but making quite a job of it this time. I have to hand it to you, and you look spectacular. Let's blow this boring party and go out somewhere."

Bren saw joy leap in his mother's eyes — saw that they shone with a fire brighter than any magic spell could light. "We could go to Arcadia," she said. "We haven't been there in years. They should have music tonight, and if they don't, we'll have a drink by the fire and go on somewhere else."

"We'll go to Arcadia," said Bob, "and then maybe we'll just go home."

Miranda reached out almost shyly and touched his face. "Home," she said. "Why didn't I think of that? What a lovely idea, Bob."

She seemed to have forgotten Alia, and this, thought Bren, was unwise in the extreme. For Alia, he now realized, was not to be trifled with. She was a woman scorned and a thwarted witch. She was furious, and she was dangerous.

At the instant that these thoughts flashed through his mind, while Bob and Miranda still gazed into each other's eyes, he saw Alia turn with a swift, serpentine movement and run down the short flight of steps from the stage. At the same moment, Erika, followed by Louise and Rose, emerged from the wings. "Louise," Bren cried, sprinting past them. "Look after Mom for a minute. I think she's lost her powers, and she's going to need them."

Bren reached the center aisle of the theater in time to see Alia moving swiftly out the back door. It never occurred to him that she might be leaving the theater. She was bent upon mischief, and she was not going to go home to concoct it, of that he was sure. But where could she have gone? He paused in the empty lobby and gazed around. The ladies' room? Was she in there, mixing some deadly brew? Not likely, and what good would it do her when neither of the objects of her rage could be persuaded to drink anything she offered? There was only one other place to look, a place as familiar to Bren as his own room. He galloped up the stairs to the balcony and stood breathless outside the door to the light booth. The padlock that Eli had snapped shut after the play was still in place. It was very still, but the atmosphere seemed charged with energy. Below him the stage shimmered with light and activity. Parents and actors clustered around the banquet table. There was Edward Bear, trapped in discourse with the great actor, and there were his mother and father, now holding hands and talking to Louise.

Suddenly, at the front of the balcony, a tall figure appeared silhouetted against the glittering stage. Bren caught his breath and slid deeper into the shadow of the light booth. Looking down the center aisle to the small open space at the rail, he could just make out the witch's white circle and triangle drawn in chalk on the dark carpeting. At least this explained Alia's seemingly magical appearance out of nowhere.

She had been down on the floor drawing the patterns that were essential to the practice of witchcraft.

Bren tried to persuade himself that his fears were groundless. He knew too much about such things to suppose that anything of far-reaching power could be accomplished in so improvised a setting. She had no thurible or athamé or wand, and above all, no time in which to summon a powerful spirit to do her bidding. Yet Bren was very much afraid. He watched the red-haired witch, who stood absolutely still within her circle, and his heart beat faster with every second that went by. He felt the strength of her hatred as if it were a palpable thing in the suffocating darkness of the balcony, and he felt the aura of power that gathered around her as she stared down at the scene below.

The stillness was broken by a low muttering as Alia began her spells. (Cabalistic garbage, Bren thought, and found that he was not in the least reassured.) Then suddenly, with a low cry she raised her arm and pointed at the stage, and in her hand was an instrument Bren had seen only once and then in a museum of anthropology. It was a twisted shaft of silvery wood, cut from a root that had grown through the body of a murdered child in its grave, carved with every symbol known to the occult world and ending in an obscene head with glaring eyes. How she had acquired such a thing or where it had been concealed were questions he could not pause to contemplate. It shone now with its own light, and the eyes blazed down through the dark theater to where Miranda stood in thrall to the ordinary magic of love.

Bren leapt like a cat down the short balcony aisle and seized Alia's arm, twisting it behind her back. He had never done such a thing before and later wondered at his sudden competence. She gave a hoarse cry and writhed free of his grasp, but the staff fell from her hand and lay on the floor, still gleaming faintly with its deathly radiance. Bren kicked it out of the circle and put his foot on it.

Alia stood for a moment staring at him, but he felt the power drain out of her, and his heart slowed. "I curse you till the day you die," she whispered. "You and your ugly mother and your stupid, stupid father. You will be sorry, Ben. So very very sorry you cannot imagine."

Bren laughed. "I think you have to get my name right to do a good job of cursing," he said, "but really, Alia, don't try anything more. I doubt my mom has retired permanently, and she's sure to be pleased with this addition to her collection." He picked up the wand and tossed it casually from hand to hand. Outside the circle of power it had lost its glow, but the sight of it, hideous and lifeless in the grasp of the smiling boy, seemed to terrify Alia. She shrank before his eyes, growing suddenly haggard and old. "You can't use it," she said. "It doesn't belong to you."

"Nor to you, I guess," Bren said. "Don't worry. Mom will probably return it to the place you stole it from, but in the meantime, I would sleep in a circle of protection every night if I were you. That will be a nuisance, but probably well worth the trouble. So, *ciao*, Alia. I'll be going now." He backed toward the stairs and then stepped hastily aside as Alia gave a horrible shriek and ran past him. He could hear her feet on the stairs and then the slam of the heavy front door of the theater.

Bren looked toward the stage, where the entire party had gathered on the apron to stare up at the balcony. Slowly and thoughtfully he went down to join them, still holding, now

208

rather gingerly, the revolting object he had wrested from his mother's rival.

Miranda pulled away from Bob at the sight of her son and the thing that he carried up onto the stage. "Where did you get it?" she cried. "Oh, Bren, put it down. You don't know what it might do."

"Don't I, though?" Bren said. "I know what I have, and it was pointed right at you! But it can't do anything now, Mom. It's just an ugly stick — ugly but interesting. I think you should hang on to it for a while just in case and then take it back to the museum."

"I'll take it back tomorrow," Miranda said. "Lou, what do you think? We don't want it around the house, do we?"

Louise reached out and took the staff from Bren. For a long moment she gazed at it reverently. "I don't know, babe," she said. "We could do a whole lot of lovely mischief, you and me. Got to think twice about giving up a thing like this."

"Give it to me and stop your nonsense," Rose snapped. "Miranda and Bob are patching it up, worse luck, and we're all back where we started from. Don't worry about that other one. We still have a clump of that fake red hair, if I'm not mistaken, enough to keep her sick for a month of Sundays if Miranda will just attend to business and stop mooning around."

"But mooning around is all I want to do right now," Miranda said, looking wistfully at Bob, who put his arm around her. "I want to go out on a date with my husband and then go home."

"And that's what you're going to do," he said, leading her off toward the exit sign.

Bren looked around at the rest of the party, most of whom had abandoned the strange scene at the front of the stage and were again gathered around the punch bowl as if it had become their only refuge in a night of baffling puzzles. Erika slipped up to his side and laid her head against his shoulder. "And what about us?" she asked. "I wouldn't mind going off into the sunset myself at this point and maybe not seeing the inside of a theater for a year or two."

"Unfortunately, we have to see it again tomorrow night," Bren said.

"Don't be so practical. I know we do, but maybe after that, we can think of something else."

"I'm thinking now," Bren said. "I'm thinking about winter and hoping it will snow, and we can build an igloo in the park, and then it will be spring, and maybe we can rent a boat."

"I'll ask my father to buy us one," said Erika.